LADY GUNSMITH

6

Roxy Doyle and the Desperate Housewife

J.R. Roberts

SPEAKING VOLUMES, LLC
NAPLES, FLORIDA
2018

Roxy Doyle and the Desperate Housewife

ISBN 978-1-62815-947-9

PART ONE

Chapter One

Roxy Doyle had been at the Sheridan Inn, in Sheridan, Wyoming for 3 days. It had comfortable accommodations, and an excellent dining room. From a porch out front she could sit in a straight-backed wooden chair, relax back against the wall, and watch the street.

The rumor that her father, Gavin Doyle, was going to be in Sheridan was what brought her there. Since the rumor had not contained a specific day, she was prepared to wait. She found the chair and its location extremely comfortable, and all she had to do was fend off advances from over-amorous cowboys every so often. That was the price she paid for being a beautiful, green-eyed redhead.

On the afternoon of the third day, she looked up as a waiter came out of the hotel carrying a mug of coffee.

"Thought you might be needin' this, Miss," he said, handing it to her.

"Thank you." He was a handsome young man she had made the mistake of sleeping with on her first night in town. She usually needed a stress reliever when she rode in off the trail. Usually she picked a man who was passing through and would be gone in the next day or so. This young man had been trying to see her again for the past two days. It even made eating in the dining room uncomfortable, but the food was so good and she didn't want to stray too far from the hotel.

"Thank you, Tommy," she said. "You're very sweet."

"I know," he said, "you said that the other night."

She'd said it while she had his cock in her hands, licking it. He was a young, sweet tasting and smelling boy. It was tempting to break her rule about sleeping with a man a second time.

"Sweet, and bad," she said. "I told you that was a one-time thing."

"I know, I know," he said, smiling, "but a boy can dream, can't he?"

"Thank you for the coffee, Tommy. You better go back to work."

"I will," he said, "but I'm not through trying."

Tommy the waiter went back inside and Roxy sat and sipped her coffee.

After she had sat in front of the hotel on the first day, she had gotten a visit from the local law . . .

***

. . . she came out to sit on the second day, and a man with a badge came from across the street.

"Marshal Kipness is my name," he said. "You're Roxy Doyle?"

"That's right."

"The one they call Lady Gunsmith?"

"I suppose."

He was in his 40s, had probably been wearing a badge for half his life

"Mind if I ask you what brings you to town?"

"This chair is pretty comfortable," she said. "This is a nice porch."

"And this is a great hotel," the marshal said. "I'll ask you again, what brought you here?"

She decided to go with the truth.

"I'm looking for my father," she said. "I heard that he was going to show up here."

"Your father?" he asked. "And who might that be?"

"A man named Gavin Doyle."

"The bounty hunter?"

"That's right."

"I thought he was dead."

"That's what they say."

"So why are you lookin' for him?" he asked. "Bounty hunters usually do the lookin'. You turnin' bounty hunter?"

"No," she said, "I'm looking for him because he's my father."

He stared at her, then said, "Doyle. I didn't put that together."

"Not a lot of people do."

"So what will you do when you find him?"

"Give him a hug and tell him I love him."

"So you have no intention of killing him?"

"No."

"Do you have any intention of killin' anyone while you're here?"

"No."

"Well, that's good," he said. "If you keep it that way, you and me won't have any trouble, at all."

"Sounds good to me, Marshal."

He seemed to accept that, and she hadn't seen him since, except in passing . . .

***

So now it was the morning of the fourth day and she was starting to wonder if she was wasting her time. Not just here in Sheridan, but all the months, years she'd spent looking for him already. Was it a fruitless search? *Was* he dead, as people had been saying? She hadn't managed to catch even the slightest glimpse of him since she'd left her foster family's care over ten years before.

But she still had a driving urge to see her father. It wasn't as if they had parted on bad terms. They had loved each other, and he had apologized for having to leave her with another family while he went off to make some money. Maybe it was no fault of his that he had never come back.

And if that was the case, she needed to know.

Chapter Two

The woman calling herself Jane Doyle got off the stagecoach in Sheridan, Wyoming on Roxy's fourth day there. In fact, Roxy saw the coach ride by in a cloud of dust kicked up by the four-horse team. But she had no idea that there was a passenger who had travelled there specifically to see her.

Jane stepped down from the stage, reached up when the driver handed down her carpetbag.

"Thank you," she said, setting the bag down. "Can you point me to the closest hotel?"

"The Sheridan Inn is just down the street," the driver said. "In fact, we passed it on the way in."

"That sounds expensive," she said.

"Well," he said, "if you walk three blocks that way you'll come to the Heritage Hotel."

"That also sounds expensive."

"Not as much as the Sheridan Inn," he told her.

"Okay," she said, "I guess that'll have to do. Thank you."

"Are you gonna need help carryin' your bag, Miss?" he asked her.

"No, thank you," she said. "I've got it."

She picked up her bag and started walking in the direction of the Heritage House. The driver watched, thinking her pretty in a simple, non-saloon girl way.

"Hey!" an impatient, male customer yelled to him. "My bag?"

***

Jane found the Heritage Hotel and checked in. As it turned out, it was affordable for her. The clerk also asked her if she needed help with her bag, but it wasn't heavy, so she told him she would take it herself.

"But you can help me with something else."

"Yes, Ma'am," the middle-aged desk clerk said. "What would that be?"

"Can you tell me who the law is here?"

"That would be Marshal Kipness."

"And where would I find him?"

"Well, if you had kept going when you came to us for one more block, you would have seen his office."

"So I go out the door and make a right?"

"Yup."

"Thank you."

She took her bag up to her room, then came back down, went out the front door, and made a right.

Jane found her way to the marshal's office and entered. The man with the badge looked up from his desk and smiled at her.

"Yes, Ma'am. Somethin' I can do for you?"

"Marshal, I just got off the stage and checked into the Heritage House."

"Okay."

"I came to town looking for someone," she said. "I heard that she was here, and I got right on the stage."

"From where?"

"Buffalo."

"Nice town."

"Usually," she said. "But not lately."

"Well, I'd like to help you, Ma'am, but I'm a town marshal. I have no authority in Buffalo."

"I understand that," she said. "I didn't come here looking for you."

"Who are you lookin' for, then?"

"A woman named Roxy Doyle," she said. "Do you know her?"

"Oh, yeah," he said. "Lady Gunsmith. She's been here for a few days."

"I heard that," she said, "so I came to see if she could help me. Can you tell me where to find her?"

"I can tell you exactly where to find her. In fact, I can take you to her."

***

Roxy watched as the marshal crossed the street toward her, leading a woman wearing a long skirt, and long-sleeved shirt that looked like travel clothes, the way women dressed to take a train, or a stagecoach. Then she remembered the stagecoach that came in just a short time earlier.

"Miss Doyle," he said, as they reached her, "I'd like you to meet—" He turned to face the woman. "I'm sorry, I didn't get your name."

"That's all right, Marshal," the woman said. "I can take it from here."

"Well . . . all right," Kipness said. "I'll say good day to you both."

He took his leave and the woman stepped up onto the boardwalk and stood there, nervously. She was an attractive woman in her mid-40s and Roxy couldn't imagine what she wanted with her.

"Can I help you with something?" she asked.

"You are Roxy Doyle, aren't you?" the woman asked. "Gavin Doyle's daughter?"

"I am," Roxy said, "but a lot of people don't know that. How did you know?"

"Your father told me," the woman said. "You see, I'm Jane Doyle—your father's wife."

Chapter Three

"My father's . . . what?" Roxy wasn't at all sure she'd heard the woman right.

"His wife?" She looked around. "Do you mind if I sit?"

"No," Roxy said. "In fact, I think you should."

There were other chairs in front of the hotel. She grabbed one and pulled it over.

"I came here from Buffalo, about forty miles away."

"That's where you live?"

"Yes," she said. "With your father."

"My father is in Buffalo?" Roxy asked, excitedly. "Right now?"

"He is," Jane said, "and that's why I'm here. I heard that Lady Gunsmith was in Sheridan."

"But . . . how did you know I was looking for him?"

"I—I didn't know that," Jane said. "How long?"

"Years," Roxy said. "Since I was fifteen years old and I left Utah."

"Utah."

Roxy nodded.

"And the family he left me with," she said.

"Were they . . . nice?" she asked.

"No, they weren't," Roxy said. "They beat me . . . tried to rape me . . . I had to get away."

"That's awful!" Jane said. "Does your father know?"

"I don't see how he could."

"Then you can tell him," Jane said. "You must come to Buffalo."

"To tell him that?" Roxy asked.

"Yes," Jane said, "and to help him. He's in trouble."

"What kind of trouble?"

"The kind that only you can help him with," Jane said. "That's why I came to find you. If you don't come back to Buffalo with me, your father . . . will be killed."

"Gavin Doyle's always been able to take care of himself, from all I've heard," Roxy said.

"Maybe not this time."

"And if he knows I'm here," Roxy went on, "why doesn't he come and see me?"

"He doesn't know you're here," she said.

"Then how did you find out?"

"I work in a millinery store," Jane said, "and a customer came in talking about how Lady Gunsmith was in Sheridan, just sitting in front of the Sheridan Inn."

"I see."

"When I heard that, I knew I had to come here and get you."

"You didn't tell my father?" Roxy asked. "Your husband?"

"No."

"Why not?"

"Because he wouldn't have let me come."

"And he would have come himself?"

"No, not that, either," Jane said.

"Why not?"

"Gavin Doyle is not the kind of man who asks for help," Jane pointed out.

"How well do you know him?" Roxy asked. "How long have you been married?"

"Only a few months," Jane said. "And we only knew each other a few months before that, so the answer is, I don't know him as well as I want to."

"But better than I do, of course," Roxy said. "How is he going to feel when I show up with you?"

"That depends on what we tell him," Jane replied. "Not that I came to ask you for help, but I came to bring you back so you could finally be with him again."

"But . . . he doesn't know I'm looking for him," Roxy said. "You didn't know that until I told you."

"That doesn't matter," Jane said quickly. "Look, I'm going to head back tomorrow. You can come with me or not. Or, you can come later. Make it look like you just happened to ride into town."

"I could do that."

"You take tonight to decide how you want to do it," Jane said, "but do it. If you don't—I'm quite desperate . . ."

"No, no, I'm going to do it," Roxy said. "I've been looking for him for a long time. Why would I not come?"

"Exactly!"

"Where are you staying?" Roxy asked.

"The Heritage House," Jane said.

"We can have supper together and talk more about you and my father."

"Oh," Jane said, "I'd like to, but I'm so tired. Why don't we wait to talk and get acquainted when you come to Buffalo?"

"Well, if that's what you—"

"Let's meet up tomorrow morning and you can tell me what you decided, whether you're gonna come with me, or come later, on your own."

"All right."

The woman was talking very quickly now, and suddenly she stood.

"This is wonderful," she said, grabbing Roxy's hands, squeezing them, then letting go. "I'll see you in the morning."

She turned and actually ran down the street, leaving Roxy behind her, puzzled.

Chapter Four

Roxy was confused.

For one thing, Jane Doyle was much younger than her father. Would he do that? Marry a younger woman? And after all the time she'd spent looking for him, would she find him settled down in a little town like Buffalo, Wyoming?

If he was there, what was he going to think when she appeared? Would he be happy to see her? Or would he be upset that Jane had come to Sheridan to find her?

But along with being confused, she was excited. After all this time, all the searching, she was finally going to see her father. She hadn't seen hide nor hair of him in all that time, except for a portrait which gave her some idea of what he looked like now.

But that was nothing compared to finally seeing him in person.

She slept fitfully that night, then went down to the Sheridan Inn dining room for breakfast. The people at the other tables, and the staff, were all used to seeing her there. And Tommy the waiter gave her extra special service.

During the meal she kept expecting to see Jane Doyle walk in, but it didn't happen. She paid her bill and had to get away from Tommy's fawning, so she left the hotel, bypassing her usual seat out front.

She walked to the Heritage Hotel, and asked the clerk what room Jane Doyle was in.

"Miss Doyle was in room five," he said.

"Thank you."

She started for the stairs, then stopped.

"Wait, you said she *was* in room five?"

"That's right."

"So she checked out?"

"Yes."

"When?"

"This morning."

"Well, obviously this morning. When this morning?"

"First thing," he said. "I came to work at seven, and she came down five minutes later."

Roxy looked at the clock on the wall. Jane had a two-hour head start, if she was heading back to Buffalo.

"Do you have any idea where she was going?"

"Home, she said."

"Was there a stage this morning?"

"Not that I know of."

"Then how would she—never mind."

Roxy left the Heritage House and went to the marshal's office. She found Kipness seated behind his desk.

"Well, good mornin', Miss—"

"Have you seen Jane Doyle this morning?"

"Jane Doy—oh, you mean the woman I introduced you to yesterday?"

"Yes. She checked out of her hotel. Do you know where she went?"

"I don't know for sure," he said, "but I'd assume she went back home to Buffalo."

"She'd have to rent something," Roxy said. "A horse, a buggy . . ."

"There are a couple of places she could do that."

"Right," Roxy said. "I'll check it out."

"Is there some reason you're, uh, after her?"

"Not the way you think," Roxy said. "I just needed to see her again."

"So, you're not—"

"—going to kill her? No, not even close. In fact, I should be leaving town very soon, myself. Maybe today."

"Well, that's good—"

Roxy didn't wait to hear the rest of the marshal's opinion.

***

She found what she wanted in the third place she looked, a small stable on a side street.

"Yes, she came in this mornin' and rented a horse and buggy," the man said.

"Did she say where she was going?"

"No," the man said, with a shrug, "I just assumed she was going out for a ride."

"I don't think so," Roxy said. "I think she was going to Buffalo."

"Buffalo!" The man looked shocked. "That's hours away. When is she gonna bring my buggy back?"

"I don't know," Roxy said. "She lives there, came in yesterday by stage."

"No, no, she can't do that," he said. "She only rented it for the afternoon."

"I don't know what to tell you," she said. "I'm going to Buffalo, though. I'll try to get her to bring it back to you, if I can."

"Well, I hope you can," he said. "I hope I don't have to go there to get it."

"You just might have to do that, Mister," Roxy said. "We all have to do things we don't want to do."

Chapter Five

Roxy decide not to try and catch up to Jane Doyle before she reached Buffalo. She simply checked out of the Sheridan Inn, collected her horse from the livery, and headed there. Once she arrived she didn't think Gavin and Jane Doyle would be so hard to find in a small town.

Little did she know . . .

***

Buffalo was much smaller than Sheridan, and she only saw one hotel on the main street, called The Occidental Hotel. She reined in her horse in front of the building, dismounted and went inside. She had covered the 40 miles in less than 4 hours, but still didn't think she had beat Jane, who had over a two-hour head start.

A tired looking desk clerk in his 40s perked up when the beautiful red-haired Roxy walked in.

"Can I help you, Ma'am?"

"First, I'd like a room."

"No problem," the man said. "We have quite a few."

"Something away from the street," she said, which was something Clint Adams, The Gunsmith, had taught her to always ask for. A room away from the street in a hotel, a table away from the window in a restaurant. "Don't ever make it easy for somebody to decide to take a shot at you," he'd also told her.

"Here ya go," the clerk said, grabbing a key. "Just sign in, please."

She wrote her real name in the registration book, left the spot for her address blank. Then she turned it around so he could read it.

"Miss Doyle," he said, handing her the key. He didn't seem to recognize her name, which suited her for the moment.

"Next you can help me by telling me where I can find Gavin and Jane Doyle."

"I'm sorry?"

"I'm looking for a woman named Jane Doyle."

He frowned.

"I don't think I know that name."

"Really? She told me yesterday that she lived here."

"Where was that?"

"We were in Sheridan."

"And she said she lived here at the hotel?"

"No," Roxy explained, "just that she lives here in Buffalo with her husband, Gavin Doyle."

"Gavin Doyle?" The man thought. "Ain't he some kinda gunman?"

"Bounty Hunter," Roxy said.

"Jeez, if they lived here in town I think I'd know it," he said. "But you could ask the sheriff."

"I will," she said. "Where would I find him?"

"His office is down the street, or he might be in the Silver Slipper Saloon."

"And where's the nearest stable?"

"We got one, all the way at the other end of the street."

"Okay, thank you."

She took her saddlebags and rifle up to her room, which had a window that overlooked an alley. She looked out, was satisfied that it was a straight drop down to the ground, with no access to her window.

Just because the hotel clerk didn't recognize Jane's name didn't mean anything. She thought he was a man, and probably never went in to a millinery.

She left the hotel and rode her horse to the livery stable, where she left it in the care of an older man who had seven fingers. She knew the other three had previously been bitten off by horses over the years, because that was often the case with men who worked with the animals.

She had passed the sheriff's office along the way, so now she walked back to it and entered. A man in his 50s was sweeping the floor, and she thought that might just be his job until she saw the battered and tarnished badge on his faded shirt.

"Can I help you, little lady?"

She hated being called "little lady" but let it go, for the moment.

"You're the sheriff?"

"Most of the time," he said. "Sheriff Greer. You look like you can handle yourself, though. Why would you need the law?"

"I'm lookin for someone."

"And you think they're here in Buffalo?"

"A woman told me she lived here with her husband," Roxy said.

"What's her name?"

"She said it was Jane Doyle."

He frowned. "Jane Doyle. I don't think I know that name."

"She said she worked in a millinery shop here."

"A what?"

"A hat store."

"Oh," he said. "Well, we have a general store, but we don't have no hat store."

"Maybe that's what she meant."

"Well," he said, scratching his balding head, "the general store's run by old man Seeger. I guess you'd have to ask him if he knows her."

"What about Gavin Doyle?" she asked.

“The bounty hunter?” he asked. “I thought he was dead.”

Chapter Six

Roxy walked to the general store, entered, saw a white-haired man behind the counter waiting on a woman with a child. The woman paid her bill, accepted her brown paper wrapped package, and then the old man gave the child a sweet as she and her mother were leaving.

"Can I help you, Ma'am?" he asked, turning his attention to Roxy. "Good God, you're beautiful."

"Thank you," Roxy said. "Are you Mr. Seeger?"

"Old Man Seeger, that's me," he said, cackling.

"Don't you have a first name?"

"I been called 'Old Man' for so long nobody remembers my first name," Seeger said. "And I don't wanna remind them." He leaned over the counter and lowered his voice. "I hate my first name." He leaned back. "What can I do for you?"

"Do you know a woman named Jane Doyle?"

"Jane Doyle," he repeated, then mulled it over. "No, I don't. Is that you?"

"No," Roxy said. "She came to me in Sheridan yesterday, told me she lived here in town and worked in a millinery shop."

"What's that?"

"A hat store."

"Well, we sell hats here," Seeger said. "But there ain't no hat store in town that I know of."

"And she doesn't work here?"

"Don't nobody work here but me," Seeger said.

"And do you know the name Gavin Doyle?"

He frowned again. "Is that a famous name? It seems to ring a bell."

"Infamous, is more like it."

He snapped his fingers. "The bounty hunter? Is that who you're talkin' about?"

"Yes."

"Ain't he dead?"

"That's what people think," Roxy said, "but I was told he lives here."

"Here? In Buffalo?"

"That's right."

"And who told you that?"

"Jane Doyle."

"The woman who said she works in a hat shop here?"

"Yes," Roxy said. "She also said she was his wife."

"Well," Seeger said. "I ain't seen neither one of them people here. But while we're at it, what's your name?"

"I'm Roxy Doyle."

"Same last name?"

She nodded. "Gavin Doyle is my father."

"And you . . . you're kinda famous, too aintcha? Or that other word? Infamous?"

"Yes," she said, "I suppose I am."

He pointed at her, as he started to get it.

"You're the one they call Lady Gunsmith, aintcha?"

"That's right."

"Are you lookin' for these people to kill them?" he asked.

"No," she said. "He's my father. I've been looking for him for years."

"And her?"

"I never met her before yesterday."

"Have you talked to the sheriff?"

"Yes," she said. "He doesn't know them either."

"Maybe she lied to you," he said. "You ever think of that?"

"If she did," Roxy said, "I still want to find her and ask her why."

"I can't say I blame ya for that," he said, "but it don't look like I can help ya much . . . that is, unless you need some supplies."

"Not right now, thanks," she said.

Two men entered and Seeger said. "I've got other customers."

"Sure," she said. "Go ahead."

She turned and started for the door, but the two men blocked her exit with thin grins on their faces. They were obviously brothers, maybe even twins.

"Hey, pretty lady, what's the hurry?" one of them asked, grinning.

"You're new in town," the other one said.

"You fellas should step aside," Roxy said. "I don't have time for this."

"Step aside, she says," one said to the other. "Whataya think?"

"You boys better do like he says," Seeger called out. "That's what I think."

"Why's that, old man?" one asked.

"Because I don't think either one of you wants to get shot by Lady Gunsmith . . . do ya?"

The young men suddenly looked at Roxy differently, fidgeting.

"Can I go now?" she asked.

"Oh, uh, sure, sure," they said, stepping aside. "We didn't mean nothin'."

"They never do," she said, and walked out.

Chapter Seven

Roxy decided to keep Gavin Doyle's name to herself. Instead, she walked around town, asking folks if they knew a Jane Doyle. When that didn't work, she started describing the woman, but still came up with nothing.

After a couple of hours of questions-and-answers, she ran into Sheriff Greer on the street.

"Sheriff," she said, "you look more like a lawman without the broom."

He was wearing a hat, his badge pinned to a vest. A gun was strapped to his waist.

"Have you had any luck with your questions?"

"None at all," she said. "I'm starting to think I was lied to, for sure."

"Well," he said, "there's one way to find out."

"And what's that?" she asked.

"You've got to go back to the beginning," he said.

"The beginning?"

"Sheridan, you said she rented a buggy to come here?"

"That's right."

"It must have left a trail," he said. "All you have to do is track her. I mean, I'm assuming you came directly here, and didn't follow her tracks."

"You're right," she said. "And you're smart."

He grinned.

"My talents involve a lot more than a broom, young lady."

She laughed.

"So I guess you came to Buffalo for nothin'," he said. "The woman wanted you to follow her."

"I guess I jumped ahead a little too far."

"Sorry I can't help you more."

"You've helped plenty," she said. "I made a big mistake, and you've pointed it out to me. I'll be leaving in the morning."

"I hope you find what you're lookin' for," Greer said.

"I've been looking a long time," she said. "I'm not about to stop now. This woman, whoever she is, made a big mistake lying to me."

"Well," Greer said, "you just make sure you let her know about it."

"Oh, don't worry," she said. "I will. Where can I get a good meal?"

"You can get a meal and a room at the same place, the Occidental. We ain't got much else."

"Well," she said, "I've got the room, so I'll get the meal."

"I'm gonna make my rounds," he said. "Then I'll probably see you in there later. I usually eat after I'm done."

"Thanks for the suggestions, Sheriff."

***

The restaurant in the Occidental was deserted when she entered from the lobby.

"Are you open?" she asked the waiter, as he approached her.

"Oh, yes, Ma'am. Just take any table."

"Thank you."

The small, 60ish man followed her as she walked to the back of the room and sat.

"Wouldn't you like somethin' close to the front?" he asked.

"No," she said, "this is fine."

"What can I get you?"

"Sheriff Greer told me he eats here every night."

"That's right. He'll be here in a little while."

"What does he usually have?"

"Most of the time he has a steak. Some nights, if the weather's cold, beef stew."

"Well," she said, "it's not cold out, but beef stew sounds good."

"Yes, Ma'am. To drink?"

"Beer."

"Comin' right up."

He turned and went through a doorway she assumed led to the kitchen. She sat back in her chair and thought about the mistakes she'd made. Jane Doyle had said she was desperate, but it was Roxy who acted that way. She should have asked Jane more questions, forced her to meet her for supper. Once she realized the woman was gone, she should have followed her trail, but she was in too much of a hurry to get to Buffalo. Now she was going to have to do what Sheriff Greer suggested: go back to Sheridan and start over.

Luckily there was no wind, no rain, to wash away her trail. It should still be there. Roxy wasn't an expert tracker, but a horse and buggy should leave a clear trail.

The waiter came back with a mug of cold beer, and then a bowl of steaming hot beef stew.

When the sheriff came in some time later, he went to a table—probably his regular table—and ordered. He looked at Roxy only once and nodded. Then the waiter appeared to bring him a bowl of beef stew. Roxy made no move to join the man. They had said all they needed to say to each other.

When she finished eating she paid, exchanged another nod with the lawman, and went to her room.

Chapter Eight

She slept fitfully, rose, washed, and went down to the desk to check out.

"After only one night?" the clerk asked.

"That's all I needed."

"Did you find the people you were looking for?"

"No."

"Then maybe you need another day?"

"No," she said. "I'm done here."

She paid her bill and went into the restaurant for breakfast. The only other person she saw eating in there was the sheriff.

"Ah, back again," the waiter said. "Same table?"

"Yes."

As they passed the lawman he looked up and nodded at her.

"Does he eat here all the time?" Roxy asked the waiter.

"The sheriff? He has breakfast before his rounds, and supper after rounds."

"Does anybody else eat here?"

"Occasionally," he said. "There really aren't a lot of people living around here, these days."

"Well," Roxy said, "I wish I'd known that before I rode over here. Ham-and-eggs, please."

"Comin' up."

***

Riding back to Sheridan she wondered why, if the woman was going to lie about living somewhere, she would choose Buffalo? And then disappear? What did she expect Roxy to do? And was she lying about being married to Gavin Doyle? She seemed like a wife desperate for some help, but she might simply have been an excellent liar.

Roxy pushed her horse harder this time, arriving in Sheridan in the afternoon. She went directly to the marshal's office and found Kipness behind his desk.

"You're back," he said, not particularly happy about it. "Did you find the woman you were lookin' for? Or your father?"

"No," she said, "I found a dead town where nobody knew who I was talking about. She obviously doesn't live there."

"Why would she do that?" he asked.

"I don't know," she said, "but I'll ask when I find her."

"So you think she's still here?"

"No," she said. "She rented a horse and buggy, I know that. I'm going to try to pick up her trail. I just wanted to check in with you, in case you saw her after I left."

"Nope," Kipness said, "I didn't. I doubt she was still in town."

"Yes, I do, too," she said. "She left but didn't go to Buffalo."

"But you did."

"That was my mistake," she said, "which I'm going to fix."

"Do you think you can pick up her trail now, a day later?"

"I'm no expert, but I hope so," she said. "But first I need a new horse."

"What's the matter with the one you've got?"

"She's a little old," Roxy said. "When I track this woman, I have no idea how far or to where it'll be. I need a horse that'll stand up to the trip."

"Well, there are a couple of places in town you can get one," he said. "Otherwise, you'll have to ride out to one of the ranches—"

"I don't have time for that," she said. "I'll get one in town. Will they trade?"

"If your horse isn't lame," he said, "you should be able to make a deal for cash and trade."

"It'll probably be the last of my cash, but I need a fit animal."

"The two places are . . ."

***

He told her where they were. Roxy realized one of them was the place where "Jane Doyle" had rented her horse and buggy. She decided she would start there. Maybe she could make a deal with the man.

"Okay," he said, after she explained her plan, "I'll take your horse, plus you'll get my horse and buggy back, in exchange for a good mount."

"I have some cash—"

"No, no," the old hostler said, "I won't need cash from you unless you can't find my horse and buggy. Bring those back to me and we'll be all even."

"But if I don't find them," she said, "what if I don't come back here?"

He studied her for a moment, then said, "You'll be back. You wanna find this woman and I get the feeling you ain't gonna stop until you do. Now, come on out back and pick out a horse."

She chose a 5-year old grey gelding that had a deep chest and long stride. The hostler transferred her saddle to it and walked it out the front door to her.

"If you have to run anybody down," he told her, "this one will do it."

Roxy knew that. This was the best horse she'd had in a while. She wasn't usually choosy about what she rode from one point to the next, as long as it got her there. This was a different situation.

"Thanks."

"I've got something else for you," he said.

"What is it?"

"Come back inside."

She tied the horse off and followed him back into the barn. He took her to a large, open spot in back.

"This is where the buggy stood," he said, pointing. "Look there."

She looked down at the ground, narrowed her eyes, and then saw what he was talking about.

"A nick?"

"A small one, in the back right wheel," he said. "That's your sign. That's what's gonna help you track your woman down. You may lose the trail at some point, but that mark will help you pick it up again."

"I appreciate that," she said. "Thanks."

"Will you be leavin' now?" he asked.

"Tomorrow," she said. "I've got to go to the general store early and pick up some supplies."

"Okay, then," he said, "I'll take Horace back inside and unsaddle him. When you get to the general store tomorrow morning, he'll be there, waitin' for ya."

"Horace?" she asked.

He nodded, said, "Horace."

Chapter Nine

Roxy followed the tracks from the stable, but only as far as the main street, where they were swallowed up by so many others. But she continued along the street and out of town and, sure enough, thanks to the old hostler, she found the tracks with the nicked wheel.

She followed the buggy tracks until it started to get dark. They were heading south, which might indicate Jane was going into Colorado. Of course, she could have been stopping somewhere before that, but for now Roxy had to camp the night.

She took better care of Horace than she ever had any other horse. Saw to his comfort and feeding before even building a fire and feeding herself. A meal of coffee and beans was good enough. It was virtually all she had purchased that morning, when she found Horace waiting for her in front of the general store as promised. Clint Adams had taught her to travel light, so coffee, jerky and beans were usually all she had in one saddlebag. The other had extra shirts, bullets, and an extra gun.

She finished her last cup of coffee while watching the night sky. Then she rolled herself up in her bedroll, with her gun nearby, and went to sleep, not feeling any necessity to keep any kind of watch, since she was the pursuer.

***

In the morning she had breakfast of coffee and a piece of beef jerky, then saddled the gelding, mounted up and started off again. The trail was hit and miss, at times getting lost when it crossed a field or an expanse of hard scrabble ground. But when she continued straight on she'd pick it up again, until late in the afternoon, when it seemed to have disappeared.

She reined in, dismounted and walked around, studying the ground. It was soft enough to have maintained the impression of the buggy, but the tracks were nowhere to be found. She could keep going straight, as she had been for some time, but if the buggy had veered off at some point, going straight would put her further and further off the mark.

She had not yet reached the Colorado border. If the buggy had changed direction, where would it go? To a nearby town? Roxy realized now she should have tried to find out exactly where Jane Doyle had caught the stage into Sheridan. That might have been helpful, but it was too late now.

She decided her only chance was to backtrack a bit and go in to the closest town. Once there she could get her bearings and make a decision.

She mounted up, turned and started to retrace her steps.

***

By the time she came to the road sign that said: FOUNDATION, 5 Miles, she still hadn't found the trail. She decided her only option was to head into town. At the very least she could replenish her supplies.

It was a bustling town, which surprised her because she had never heard of it before. And because it was bustling, there was a myriad of tracks leading into town, pounding each other into the dirt and out of existence. If Jane Doyle's buggy had been there at any point, the proof was long gone.

Roxy located the general store, figuring if Jane had changed direction it might have been for supplies.

She went inside, waited her turn and asked for a couple of cans of beans and some coffee.

"Have you had any strangers in to buy supplies?" she asked the clerk.

The young man had been eyeing her since she came in and had nervously asked if he could help her. He was no less nervous when he responded.

"Only you," he said, his eyes wide as he stared at the beautiful face across the counter from him.

"No other women? Maybe driving a buggy?"

"No, Ma'am," he said. "S-sorry, Ma'am, but only you. A fella or two been in, just passin' through, but no other women. Only—"

"—I know," she cut him off. "Only me."

"Y-yes, Ma'am."

"Who's the law in town?"

"That'd be Sheriff Melville. His office is right on our main street, a coupla blocks from here."

"Thank you."

She paid for her supplies, took them outside and stowed them in her saddlebags, then took her horse's reins and walked the animal to the sheriff's office.

Chapter Ten

There was nobody in the sheriff's office, but as she left she saw a man wearing a badge crossing the street toward the office.

"Lookin' fer me?" he asked.

"I am if you're the sheriff."

"Sheriff Melville, at your service, Ma'am," he said, touching the brim of his hat. "Why don't we go inside?"

She followed him in. He was tall and well-built for a man who looked about 50 years old. He had a grey moustache matched by the gray hair she saw as he took off his hat and hung it on a wall peg.

He sat behind his desk and asked, "Now, what can I do for ya, Miss . . ."

"I'm tracking a woman in a buggy, and lost her trail nearby,"

Roxy said. "I thought she might've come into town for supplies, or maybe a telegraph office."

"You law?"

"No, sir."

"Bounty hunter?"

"No."

"Then why are you trackin' this woman?"

"Because she lied to me, and I want to find out why."

"You didn't tell me your name."

"It's Doyle, Roxy Doyle."

The sheriff sat back and looked at her.

"Lady Gunsmith?"

"That's right." More and more people were recognizing her name immediately, and it was just something she was going to have to get used to. She hadn't been carrying the moniker around for as long as Clint Adams, and he had certainly come to terms with it.

"And you're only after this woman because she lied to you?" he asked. "You're not after her for . . . some other reason? Like killin' her?"

"Not at all," Roxy said. "She told me she knew something about my father. I've been looking for him for years."

"Who's your father?"

Roxy had never talked about this so much within so few days.

"Gavin Doyle," she said, "and don't say you thought he was dead."

Those very words had been on their way out of his mouth and he snatched them back.

"Well," he said instead, "I won't ask any more questions, because I don't think I can add anythin' that would help your search. Strangers don't come through here often, and sure as hell not women traveling alone." He frowned. "Is she traveling alone?"

Now it was Roxy's turn to frown. "She was."

***

As she left the sheriff's office she wondered if Jane changed directions to join up with someone? Her father? But if so, why wouldn't her father have just come to Sheridan after hearing she was there? And why was Jane running from her?

Then she started thinking, maybe the woman wasn't running from her. Maybe she was leading her somewhere. After all, the trail she had left—to this point, anyway-was not difficult to follow. If she *didn't* want Roxy to follow her, she would have taken steps to hide it.

So the reasonable assumption was, the trail was still out there. Roxy had simply missed it.

Her stop in Foundation had yielded her some supplies, and the confirmation that she was still heading in the right direction.

She just had to try harder to find the trail, and Jane Doyle.

Chapter Eleven

She rode back out to the point where she felt she had lost the trail. It would be dark in an hour, but she dismounted and started walking, leading the horse behind her. She was almost ready to give up when she saw it. The buggy had veered off, not to go to Foundation, but to head west. It may have been possible that Jane was heading for Idaho, rather than Colorado.

Roxy camped for the night, secure in the knowledge that she had found the trail again and would be back on Jane's tail in the morning.

***

Jane Doyle rolled over in bed and looked at her husband's bare butt as he lay on his belly. She ran her hand down the line of his back, trailed one finger up and down the crease between his butt cheeks. They were not youngsters, but they enjoyed sex, and as soon as she had arrived he had taken her to bed. Now she was pleasantly fatigued from both her trip, and the sex, but certainly not done.

While he dozed she suspended herself over him so that the nipples of her full breasts lightly brushed his back. Then she moved down to his lower back and, eventually, the full, rounded globes of his butt.

Jane considered herself a modern woman. Sex was one of the things she had adopted a modern attitude about. There wasn't anything she wouldn't do in bed for her man.

As she ran her nipples over the backs of his thighs, she set her cheek against his butt cheek, enjoying the heat of him on her face, and scent of him in her nostrils. Then, as she began to run her tongue up and down that crease between his cheeks, he stirred.

"What are you about, woman?" he asked.

"Pleasing my man," she said, with her face nestled between his ass cheeks.

Abruptly, he rolled over, and his hard cock appeared right in front of her face.

"Then start pleasing me from the front, not the back," he said.

"My pleasure," she said, and took his hard penis into her mouth . . .

***

"Jesus, woman!" he said, a little later, "You tryin' to kill me?"

"Just tryin' to wake you up and keep you happy, my husband," she replied.

"We ain't talked since you got back, for all the fuckin'," he said. "So before I make *you* happy tell me . . . is she gonna come?"

"Don't worry," she said, "she'll come."

"How can you be so sure?"

"Because I lied to her," Jane said. "She ain't gonna stand for that. She's gonna want to find me and demand to know why."

"But you steered her to Buffalo."

"That's all part of it," she said, lying on her back next to him. "She'll go to Buffalo, then back to Sheridan. By the time she discovers that I lied, and left a trail, she'll follow it."

"I hope you didn't make the trail too easy to follow," the man said, sliding his hand down over her belly. "We don't want her to become suspicious."

"She's gonna be too mad, and too curious, to be suspicious," she assured him, as her husband's fingers dipped into her. She gasped and arched her back as he began to stroke her.

"Then I guess it's my turn to make you happy," he said, leaning down to replace his fingers with his aggressive mouth . . .

***

Breathlessly, Jane Doyle gasped out, "Now that's what I call pleasin' a woman!"

"This ol' dog still knows his ol' tricks," her husband said.

He got up off the bed and walked naked to the window to look down at the street.

"They're not here, yet, darlin'," Jane said.

"You never know," he said. "They might just sneak into town."

"All eight of 'em?" she asked.

"Or maybe one at a time," he said, turning to look at her. "You know, I could handle them one at a time."

"*We* could handle 'em one at a time," she said, "but you know they ain't got the gumption for that."

"Yeah, I know." He turned, walked back to the bed. They were both middle-aged, their bodies giving in to the passage of time, and yet they only saw love and beauty when they looked at each other.

He stared down at her, full breasts no longer as high as they had once been, her middle and thighs thicker, and thought he had never seen anything so lovely.

She looked up at him, the muscle tone in his chest and arms showing signs of wear, his relaxed penis hanging from a tangle of grey hairs between his legs.

They had found each other several months earlier and were happier than they had ever been.

He got back in bed with her.

"I hope this works," he said.

"Of course it will work," she said. "She's been looking for Gavin Doyle for a long time. I was lucky enough to hear somebody talking about her being in Sheridan. This is fate. All I had to do was bait the hook."

"You really believe that?" he asked. "I mean, in fate and such?"

She put her head on his shoulder, pressed her body tightly to his.

"What else could it be?" she asked. "Fate has brought us all together for a reason."

"The death of five men?" he asked.

She kissed his shoulder and tried to snuggle even closer to him.

"That's the reason."

Chapter Twelve

Roxy picked up Jane Doyle's trail again, determined this time not to lose it. But as the day went on, just riding and reading the sign on the ground, it seemed more and more Jane Doyle was doing nothing to hide her trail. Alone with her thoughts, Roxy started to think that she was definitely playing into someone's hands. It was fairly obvious she wasn't being watched, but that didn't mean she wasn't being waited for.

But she decided to continue on her chosen path. Wherever the trail finally led her, she was going to approach it with caution. Not only did she not like the idea that Jane Doyle had lied to her, but that she was now manipulating her. It would have served the woman right if Roxy turned around right now and rode away. The only problem with that was, Jane still might actually be married to Gavin, and leading Roxy to her father. She couldn't take the chance that if she rode away, she'd be riding away from her father.

So she continued on . . .

***

Roxy made camp as it got dark, cared for her horse, built a fire, had supper, and went to sleep. In the morning she took the time to prepare herself a hot breakfast of freshly made hard tack. Carefully she poked holes in the biscuits and covered the pan to let them finish. Since she was now convinced that Jane Doyle was waiting somewhere for her, she decided to let her wait.

After 30 minutes the hard tack was ready. She sat at her fire and ate it, washing it down with strong coffee—the strong trail coffee she had learned to like and make from the Gunsmith, Clint Adams.

Finished with breakfast she doused the fire, stowed her gear, saddled her horse and went out after Jane Doyle's trail. There it was, clear as day, but she still had no idea where it was leading her.

And the question that was still nagging at both the back and front of her mind was—why?

She was growing tired of asking herself the same questions over and over again. Instead of letting her thoughts continue to repeat themselves, she decided to concentrate on what she was going to do when she finally caught up to Jane.

If she was, indeed, married to Gavin Doyle, she would put her feelings about Jane aside and talk to him. On the other hand, if Jane was not married to her father, she was going to make her pay.

***

As determined as Roxy was to track Jane Doyle down, her resolve and confidence wavered as she realized the woman could be headed for either Idaho Territory, or Utah Territory. She had no desire to cross from Wyoming to Utah. She had taken her leave of the territory of Utah when she was 15 and vowed never return. And why would her father go back after all this time? The answer was, he wouldn't. The question that remained now was, would she follow Jane Doyle there?

***

The answer came fairly quickly, when Roxy saw the wagon trail cross the border from Wyoming Territory into Idaho Territory. With a deep sigh of relief, she followed.

What was in Idaho?

All she knew was, Jane Doyle had gone there.

No more questions. Now that she was committed, she would ask herself no more questions.

***

By the time she realized she was being followed, they were almost on her. She turned in her saddle and saw them in the distance—Indians.

There was a band of them, and they were riding hard enough to kick up dust. She knew the Bannock were indigenous to the area, and that they were connected to the Shoshone. She also knew they had been put on a reservation after the Bannock War a few years earlier. But she had no way of knowing if these riders were reservation Bannock, or Bannock who had left and gone renegade.

And she didn't want to find out.

Before they reached her she spurred her horse into a hard gallop and tried to put distance between herself and the Indians.

She knew the Bannock of the reservation made pottery and jewelry, but if these were those people, why would they be riding so hell-bent-for-leather? Unless they themselves were being chased.

That could be it. The only way to find out was to take cover and see if they would ride right past her. But she had to be out of their sight—even for an instant—before she could do that.

And she had to do that before they caught up to her.

Chapter Thirteen

The ground around her was flat, and the Bannock horses were good ponies. Luckily, for once she had spent the extra for a good horse, and the animal was keeping the distance between her and the Bannock fairly even.

But eventually the road came to an area lined with rocks. As she followed the bend she saw an opening between two large boulders. Quickly, she jerked her reigns and guided the horse through the gap. The animal was almost too wide to get in, but finally managed. She dismounted, put her hand over the horse's nose and mouth to calm him and keep him quiet.

The Bannock rode by, none of them looking her way, which suited her. She had no desire to start killing Indians, but she remained prepared to draw her gun, if necessary.

She stayed secreted between the two boulders until she could no longer hear hoof beats of the Indian ponies. When they had faded away, she walked out with her horse and looked around. There were no Bannock in sight, and none within earshot. She mounted up, hoping that the Indian ponies had not stamped out Jane Doyle's trail.

She had to ride for a few miles before the multiple unshod hoof prints of the Indian ponies broke off from the wagon wheel trail left by Jane. She breathed a sigh of relief that they were all no longer going in the same direction. In fact, the Bannock may not even have been pursuing her. They could have been running themselves, or simply in a hurry to get somewhere.

She didn't care, as long as it was somewhere she wasn't going.

***

Roxy had never been in Idaho Territory before. It was north of the Utah Territory, where she had spent some of her formative years, but when she left at 15 she did not go north, she went east.

She reigned her horse in 3 miles outside a town called Paris, Idaho. The tracks of Jane's wagon seemed to be headed right for it. She decided not to follow the tracks into town. Instead, she circled the town and came at it on a road coming from the opposite side. She did not see any of the wagon tracks leaving town, so if Jane Doyle had driven it into town, she had not driven out.

In the wagon, anyway.

She followed the road into Paris.

It was a small town on the west side of Bear Lake. The buildings were old and sparse, yet there was a two-story hotel that looked fairly new. There was also a livery stable, which was what she needed.

She rode right down the middle of town, because there was no other way. And if Jane Doyle wanted Roxy to follow her all this way, then she might as well let the woman see her.

When she reached the livery stable, she stopped in front and dismounted. No one came out to see what she wanted, so she walked in. It was large, with a lot of empty stalls. But one stall in the back had a horse in it, and also sitting in the rear of the barn was a buggy.

"Can I help you?" a voice asked, from behind her.

She turned, saw a tall, thin man facing her. In his 40s, he wore faded jeans and a threadbare shirt, and on his chest was a makeshift badge.

"Can you tell me who that buggy belongs to?" she asked.

"Why should I do that?"

"Because," she said, "I followed it here from Sheridan, Wyoming."

"That buggy?" he asked. "You followed that buggy?"

"Yes."

"How do you know it's that one?"

She pointed to the ground, where the wagon had left its wheel marks. Then she went down to one knee and touched the ground.

"That nick," she said. "I followed that nick all the way here."

She stood up.

"You're the sheriff?" she asked. "The real sheriff?"

He smiled.

"Don't let the badge fool you," he said. "I'm the deputy, and I own this stable. My name's Andy Smith. That wagon belongs to a woman."

"Jane Doyle," Roxy said. "At least, that's how she introduced herself to me in Sheridan."

"Are you trackin' her to arrest her?"

"I'm not the law."

"To kill her, then?"

"No."

"Then why?"

"I want to ask her some questions."

"What questions?"

"I want to know why she lied to me."

"And?"

"And," Roxy said, "if she really is my step-mother."

The deputy smiled. She thought he had a nice one.

Chapter Fourteen

While Deputy and Hostler Andy Smith unsaddled Roxy's horse for her he said, "The woman came in here with that buggy a couple of days ago. The horse was kind of stove up, and she said she was gonna be stayin' here for a while."

"Did she say she was meeting someone here?" she asked.

"No," Smith said, "but I figured."

"Why's that?"

He turned and looked at her, holding her saddle in his hands.

"Why else would someone come here, unless they're lookin' for someone?"

He turned and set her saddle down, then took the blanket off her horse.

"I'll rub him down and feed him for you. Looks kind of stove up, too."

"We both are."

"Well, we got one hotel in town, pretty new," he said. "That woman is there, too."

"Thanks."

"You wanna tell me your name before you go over there?" he asked.

"Roxy Doyle."

"Uh-huh," he said, "and you say she's Jane Doyle?"

"That's right."

"Married to your pa?"

"That's what she claimed."

"And he would be?"

Roxy hesitated.

"Gavin Doyle."

He frowned.

"The bounty man?"

"That's right."

"I thought he was—and he's your pa?" he said, catching himself before saying he thought he was dead.

"He is."

"Damn," he said, "that sorta makes you the Lady Gunsmith, don't it?"

"It does."

"I heard you was lookin' for him."

She knew her legend had gotten around, but not that she was looking for Gavin. If that was the case, then her pa must have heard it, too. Why would he then not come looking for her? Or, at least, try to let her know where he was. Or, failing all of that, just stay put somewhere so she could find him?

"So are you tellin' me he might be here in Paris?" Smith asked.

"That's what I'm hoping," she said.

"Well, for your sake I hope you're right," he said, "but for the town's sake, I hope you ain't."

Roxy knew what he meant. What lawman would want not only Lady Gunsmith in his town, but bounty hunter Gavin Doyle, as well? That was just looking for trouble.

"Well," she said, "if I find him, I'll do you a favor and get me and him out of your town, pronto."

"I appreciate that, Ma'am."

"I'll head over to the hotel now to see what I can find out."

"That's fine," he said. "I'll be seein' to your animal, so you'll be able to find me either here, or in my office."

"Okay."

"Failin' that," he said, "try The Grizzly."

"The Grizzly?"

"The Grizzly Bear Saloon," he said. "Cold beer and good steaks. I usually have my supper there, with the sheriff."

"Okay, Deputy," she said, "thanks."

***

When not in bed with her man, Jane Doyle spent most of her time looking out of the window, waiting for Roxy Doyle to come riding down the street. So she was surprised that day when Lady Gunsmith came riding in from the opposite direction.

"She's here?"

"What?" he asked, from the bed where he had been napping.

"She's ridin' in now," Jane said.

Her man quit the bed and rushed over to the window, standing next to her.

"That's her?"

"See that red hair, and the gun?" Jane asked. "That's her."

"We better get down there—"

"No," Jane said, grabbing his arm to keep him from running out the door. "I'll go."

"But—"

She tightened her hold on his arm and said, "We don't wanna take a chance of anybody seein' you on the street. Not when we've come this far."

"You're right," he said. "All right, my sweet. You go down and see 'er. I'll wait here."

"Don't worry," she said, "I'll bring 'er to you."

She rushed to the door, opened it, then turned and said to him, "And let's hope she don't just kill us both."

Chapter Fifteen

Above the front entrance of the hotel was a sign that just read HOTEL. As Roxy approached it, Jane Doyle came walking out. Roxy was elated that she wasn't going to have to keep looking for the woman. It was also encouraging that Jane smiled as she approached. Galling, but encouraging.

"Hello, Roxy," Jane said.

"You've led me a merry chase," Roxy said.

"I thought I left you a pretty clear trail to follow," Jane said.

"You did. I caught on pretty quick that you actually wanted me to find you."

"I did," Jane said, "and I'm sorry."

"Why didn't you just tell me what you wanted?" Roxy asked her.

"I didn't want to take a chance you'd say no," Jane said.

"Where is he?"

"He's in a room upstairs," Jane said, "but before we go up—"

"Just take me."

"Roxy, I have to tell you—"

"Just take me up, Jane!"

Jane hesitated a moment, then said, "Yes, all right. Come on."

She led Roxy into the hotel, up the stairs, and across the hall. Then she stopped in front of room 5.

"Over the street?" Roxy asked.

"We wanted to be able to watch for you out the window," Jane said.

"So that means . . ." Roxy said.

Jane used her key to open the door. The man by the window turned and looked at them as they entered. He was average height, looked to be in his 50's, wearing trail clothes. And he was barefoot.

He wasn't Gavin Doyle.

"You don't look surprised," he said.

"I started to suspect," she answered. "Then when I realized what room you were in, I knew. My father would never take a room over the street."

"I'm sorry," he said. "I—we—were desperate."

"Are you two even married?" Roxy asked.

"Yes, we are," Jane said, rushing to her husband's side. "Happily."

"Is your name Doyle?"

"No," the man said. "My name's John Billings."

"And you?"

"I'm Jane Billings."

"And I'm here why?"

"Because we need help," Jane said. She and her husband exchanged a look. "Badly," she added.

"Why didn't you just ask?" Roxy said.

"I couldn't," Jane said. "I would've just been a stranger asking you for help. Why would you do it?"

"We'll never know the answer to that," Roxy said, "but why should I do it now?"

She turned and left the room.

***

Roxy got down to the street, stopped right in front of the hotel, wondering what to do next. Leave town? Forget all about these people? What kind of trouble were they in?

No, she didn't care what kind of trouble they were in. She didn't know them. The woman had lied to her, made her go to Buffalo, back to Sheridan, and all the way to Paris, Idaho.

Paris.

Idaho!

And for what?

She'd never know.

Could she live with that? Never knowing what had brought her all this way?

Before she could decide, Jane Billings came running out of the hotel behind her. She stopped short when she saw Roxy just standing there.

"Please, Miss Doyle!" she shouted.

Roxy turned.

"I'm desperate," Jane said. She reached out, as if to grab Roxy by the shoulders, but then pulled her hands back. "Just give me a chance to plead my case."

Roxy stared at the woman. She was still angry about the lies, but she couldn't dismiss the fact that she was curious. And she had come all this way, followed and lost and followed Jane's trail, avoided Bannocks, and followed the trail again from Sheridan, Wyoming to Paris, Idaho.

Idah—

She shook her head, telling herself to stop doing that.

"Okay," she said, "I'm going to listen . . ."

"Thank you."

". . . but I'm starting out angry with you, so I don't think I'm going to end up helping you."

"I'm just happy that you're going to listen."

"But not here," Roxy said.

"Then where?"

Roxy thought, then said, "The Grizzly."

Chapter Sixteen

"There are five of them," Jane said, "and they mean to kill my husband."

"Who are they?"

"The leader's name is Hitch Moran," Jane said. "The other four just do whatever he tells them to do. It's not even always the same four."

"So why doesn't your husband have it out with him?" Roxy asked.

"Well first, because it's never just Hitch, it's always five of them."

"He always has four men with him?"

"Yes."

"And second?"

"John isn't a gunman," Jane said. "Even if he stood in the street with just Hitch, he'd get killed."

"And how's Hitch with a gun?"

"Fast," Jane said. "John says he's the fastest he's ever seen—and he once saw Hickok."

"And the four men with him?"

"They're usually gun hands," Jane said. "Not fast guns. John had to explain the difference to me."

They were professional guns, though not necessarily fast with them. But they could hit what they aimed at.

"So," Roxy said, "is Hitch coming here?"

"Hitch is lookin' for Johnny," Jane said. "Right now, he doesn't know we're here."

"And how did you know I was in Sheridan?"

"This town is so small that I had to ride to a bigger one to get some supplies," she said. "While I was there someone came in from the other direction. They mentioned you and Sheridan and that you were there looking for your father."

Roxy didn't like that.

"Something wrong?" Jane asked.

"I didn't know word about me got around that much," she said.

"But . . . you're Lady Gunsmith."

"I know that," Roxy said. "I just didn't realize that people knew what I was doing."

"I can see where it would be a problem," Jane said, "but it gave me the idea to, uh . . ."

"Lie to me?"

". . . ask you for help."

"By lying to me."

"I—well, like I told you, I—I just thought you wouldn't listen to me."

Roxy looked around the Grizzly. A few men were lined up at the bar, some of the tables were occupied by people eating steak dinners—which was the only thing the Grizzly prepared.

"Will you help us?" Jane asked.

"You still haven't given me a good enough reason."

"To keep Johnny from bein' killed," Jane said. "That's the only reason I have."

"You not only lied to me," Roxy said, "you made me think I had a good chance of finding my father."

"I'm sorry about that," Jane said. "Did I tell you I was desperate?"

"Let me ask you something," Roxy said. "If I help you, and Hitch is no longer looking for Johnny, will that be the end of it?"

"What do you mean?"

"You haven't told me why Hitch wants to kill your Johnny," Roxy pointed out.

"I—didn't think it was important."

"It's very important," Roxy said. "Does Johnny do things, or say things, that make people want to kill him? If Hitch goes away, will someone else just take his place? I won't be around to save Johnny every time. So why should I do it now?"

Jane sat back in her chair and put her fork down.

"I can't tell you that."

"Why not?"

"That would be for Johnny to decide if he wants to tell you."

"Well then, let's go and ask him."

"First I have to order him a steak," Jane said.

"Do you bring all his food to the room?"

"Yes. He doesn't wanna be seen on the streets. Just in case."

"I guess I can sympathize with that," Roxy said. "Being seen on the street is not always a good idea."

"I'll order his steak dinner, and then we can go back to the hotel."

"And will he tell me what this is all about?"

"To tell you the truth," she said, "I don't know if he will or not."

"Is it that bad?"

"I don't know," she said, "because he's never told me about it."

Chapter Seventeen

The two women walked back to the hotel, found Johnny Billings sitting on the bed.

"Hello, Ladies," he said, smiling. "Are we all set?"

"Not quite," Jane said. "Roxy wants to talk to you."

"Oh?" Billing said, not looking happy.

"Yeah, she'd like to know—"

"Jane," Roxy said, "can I talk to Johnny alone?"

"Alone?"

Roxy nodded.

"Here? In the room?"

"Yes."

"With you?"

"Jane," Roxy said, "I just want to talk to him."

"Yeah, honey," Johnny said, standing up, "why don't you let me and Roxy talk?"

"Okay," she said. "I'll be in the Grizzly."

"Alone?" Johnny asked.

"I'll be fine," she said. "I'll talk to you both later."

Jane reluctantly left the room, closing the door with a slam.

"She gets jealous," Billings said.

"Does she have reason to get jealous?" Roxy asked.

"Well . . . women kind of like me."

"Really? Why?"

Billings looked hurt.

"Never mind," Roxy said. "I don't need to know any of that. And she doesn't have anything to fear from me."

"Right," Billings said.

She took a good look at him for the first time. He was certainly old enough to be her father, but looked nothing like him. He was rugged looking, though, and might appeal to some women.

"How long have you and Jane been married?" she asked.

"Huh? Oh, a few months."

"Do you love her?"

"What? Of course I love 'er."

"As much as she loves you?" Roxy said. "Because she's certainly gone a long way for you."

"I know that," Billings said. "I was worried sick thinking somethin' might happen to her."

"Why? Does this man Hitch know about Jane?"

"Jesus, I hope not," Billings said.

"Well, he will if he catches up to you, and the two of you are together."

"Yeah, yeah," he said, running his hand through his hair, "I understand."

"So tell me, Johnny," Roxy said. "Why does this fella Hitch want you dead?"

Billings frowned and went to the window.

"Not a good idea to stand in front of the window," Roxy said.

"Yeah, right." He moved away.

"How have you stayed alive this long?" she asked.

"By runnin'," he said, "and hidin'. But I ain't proud of it."

"So you've done it before?"

"All my life."

"People have been trying to kill you all your life?"

"Sometimes it seems that way."

"Well, let's deal with this one."

"That's what I'm tryin' to do," he replied.

"Why?"

"Because I don't wanna die."

"No," Roxy said, "I mean, why does he want to kill you? Jane told me you haven't even told her that."

"Yeah, well . . ."

"If you want me to help," Roxy said, "or even consider helping, you'll have to tell me."

He hesitated, as if thinking it over.

"Would you have to tell Jane?"

"I'd think so, yeah," Roxy said. "But you should actually tell her."

"Yeah, I know."

"Why haven't you?"

"I don't know, really."

"This isn't getting us anywhere, Johnny."

"Then wait," he said, sticking his hand out. "Wait. Let me show you somethin'."

He hurried to the bed, reached beneath it and came out with a saddlebag. When he reached into it he came out holding several stacks of money, neatly stacked and banded.

"I can pay you."

"Wha—"

"Five thousand? Ten?"

"How much money do you have there?" she asked.

"Well . . . fifty thousand in this saddlebag."

"And?"

"Um, fifty thousand in the another one."

"And how many saddlebags are there?"

"Just the two."

"And why do I think," Roxy said, "these saddlebags belong to Hitch?"

Chapter Eighteen

"I stole it."

"I kind of figured that out," Roxy said.

"Well, I stole it from Hitch," Johnny said, "and he stole it from a bank."

"Were you part of the bank robbery?"

"No!" Johnny said. "I would never rob a bank. That was Hitch and his gang."

"Where did it happen?"

"Bullhead City, Arizona," Johnny said. "It was a small bank, but for some reason they had this payroll money, and Hitch heard about it."

"So he robbed it."

"Right."

"And you robbed him."

"Right again," Johnny said. "But . . . he's really the one who broke the law, right?"

"Stealing is against the law, Johnny," Roxy said. "I don't think it really matters who you steal from."

"Oh," Johnny said, "Well, I guess you're right."

"So why haven't you told Jane?"

"I wanted to surprise her," he answered. "See, I took the money so I can buy her the home she's always wanted."

"That is, if Hitch doesn't kill you first."

"Right."

"Did it ever occur to you to return the money to the Bullhead City Bank?"

He frowned. "No."

"I'm sure they'd give you a reward," Roxy said. "Probably enough to buy that home."

"But . . . this is a hundred-thousand-dollars, Miss Doyle," Johnny said. "If I return it to the bank and they gave me, say, a ten-thousand-dollar reward, and then Hitch found me and killed me, well then, I'd die for ten thousand dollars instead of a hundred thousand. Doesn't sound worth it, does it?"

"I guess that's one way of looking at it," she said, "How is Jane going to feel about stolen money buying her the home she wants?"

"I was hopin' I could explain it so that it made sense," he said.

"Uh-huh."

"Does it make sense to you?"

She thought a moment.

"You know," she said, "I think I can see where it makes sense to you."

"But . . ."

"It's stolen money, Johnny."

"So you don't want me to pay you?"

“No.”

He shrugged, put the money back in the saddlebag, and shoved it under the bed, and then sat down, his shoulders slumped.

“So how do I get you to help me, Miss Doyle?” he asked.

“Roxy,” she said. “Call me Roxy. How do you want me to help you, Johnny? Should we put the word out that you’re here, and wait for Hitch to show up? Or should we go and find him?”

“I have a place picked out for this home for Jane,” he said. “We could go there, buy it, settle there, and wait.”

“All three of us?” she asked. “Living in the same place?”

“Um . . .”

“And what do you want me to do? Lie in wait for Hitch and then what? Kill him?”

He frowned. “I ain’t thought that far. But it was Jane’s idea to ask you. Maybe she has a plan?”

“Then maybe we should ask her.”

His face brightened and he looked up at her.

“Then you’ll help us?” he asked.

“Let’s talk to Jane first before I decide,” Roxy said.

“You mean . . .”

“Yes,” she said. “It’s time to tell Jane what it’s all about.”

***

Roxy and Johnny left the hotel and walked over to the Grizzly.

"You mean, go out?" Johnny asked, when Roxy proposed that they do that."

"I doubt Hitch is roaming the streets—or street—of this town, looking for you," she said.

"Yeah, you're probably right."

When they walked in they saw Jane sitting at a table with a beer in front of her. She was the only woman sitting alone. But the men around her weren't paying any attention to her—especially not after Roxy walked in. They all watched Roxy as she and Johnny walked to Jane's table.

When Jane saw them, her eyes widened.

"Johnny! You're takin' a chance—"

"Like Roxy said," he pointed out. "Hitch ain't here lookin' for me—yet."

"W-what are ya doin' here?" Jane asked them both.

"We need to talk, Jane," Roxy said. "And by that I mean, Johnny has something to tell you."

Jane looked at Johnny, who seemed at a loss for words.

"We better sit down," Roxy suggested.

Chapter Nineteen

"Should we be talking here?" Jane asked. "Out in the open?"

"I think so," Johnny said. "It's probably time for me to stop hidin'."

Jane looked at Roxy. "Is this your idea?"

"No," Roxy said. "I have nothing to do with it."

"Actually, you do," Johnny said. "Talkin' to you is what made me realize it."

Jane smiled at Roxy. "So you're gonna help?"

"I haven't decided yet," Roxy said. "I told Johnny first he has to tell you what this is all about."

"What it's all about?" Jane asked, looking at Johnny.

"Roxy wants me to tell you why Hitch is after me," Johnny said. "I guess, depending on how you react, she'll decide whether to help us or not."

"I'm going to the bar and get a beer," Roxy said. "When I come back, I'll bring you both one, too."

"Okay," Johnny said.

Roxy got up and walked to the bar, where the heavily bearded bartender looked at her from behind all his hair with startling blue eyes.

"Help ya?" he asked.

"I'd like a beer, please."

"Just one?"

"One for now," she said. "Thanks."

"No problem."

He brought her a mug and she sipped from it while watching Johnny and Jane talk. Johnny kept speaking very quickly, and Jane seemed to be taking the news pretty well. Finally, they both looked over at her and Johnny stopped talking.

"Bartender?" Roxy called. "Three more?"

"Sure," he said. "I can bring them over, if you want."

That was the first time Roxy noticed there were no saloon girls in the Grizzly. And she also noticed that the bearded bar man reminded her very much of a grizzly bear.

"That'd be great," she said. "Thanks."

She walked back over to the table and sat.

"The bartender brings three beers over."

"Then we can drink to celebrate that you're gonna help us," Jane said.

"You're okay with this, Jane?" she asked.

"I know Johnny never should've done what he did, but it's over. He did it. I don't think he should die because of it, do you?"

"No, I don't."

"And I'm so sorry for lying to you, Roxy," she said. "And . . . and using your father the way I did. But like I told you a couple times already—"

"—I know," Roxy cut her off. "You were desperate."

"And I still am."

"I understand that."

"Roxy," Johnny said, "I think just talkin' to you has helped a lot. And I appreciate you even talking to me after findin' out that Jane, well, lied to you."

"Okay," Roxy said, "let's forget about that, for now."

"Right," Jane said to Johnny, "let Roxy decide whether she wants to help us or not just . . . well, because."

"Right," Johnny said.

The bartender came over and set their beers down, then looked into Roxy's eyes with those piercing blues of his. She felt something flutter inside of her, and then he turned and left.

"If I decide to help you," Roxy said, "where would this help take place?"

Johnny and Jane looked at each other.

"I mean," Roxy said, "is Hitch actually out looking for you, or is he somewhere we can find him?"

"Hitch has men out looking for Johnny," Jane said. "But he stays in Arizona."

"Arizona?" Roxy asked. "Not the same town where he robbed the bank?"

"No," Johnny said, "but not that far away, either."

"So, where is he?"

"Flagstaff," Jane said.

"Flagstaff is kind of a big town," Roxy said.

"Yeah," Jane said, "he needs the telegraph office there to keep in touch with his men."

"So how many men does he have out looking?"

"Who knows?" Johnny asked. "Half a dozen? Maybe even a dozen?"

"That many?" Roxy asked. "And are they friends, or do they work for him?"

"A little bit of both," Johnny said.

"So then there's no danger of Hitch just riding into town," she said.

"Only if he finds out Johnny's here," Jane said. "No, he's going to sit in Flagstaff and wait to hear."

"Okay then," Roxy said, nodding, "we know where to find him."

"And why would we want to find him?" Jane asked, shaking her head as if to dispel the thought. "We don't want him to find us, so why would we go to Flagstaff?"

"Because," Roxy said, "that's where Johnny is going to stand up to him."

Johnny and Jane both said, "What?"

Chapter Twenty

"What the hell are you talkin' about?" Jane asked. "When I asked you to help, I thought that you . . . well, you know."

"You thought I'd kill Hitch?"

"Well, yeah," Jane said.

"My gun isn't for hire, Jane," Roxy said.

"Then what can you do for us?" Jane asked.

"I can teach Johnny what he needs to know to get rid of Hitch."

Johnny and Jane exchanged a glance, and then Johnny said, "Well uh, Roxy, you are kinda young—"

"You think because I'm younger than you I can't teach you what's needed?" she asked. "So you just thought I'd go out there and gun Hitch down?"

"That's what I hoped you'd do," Jane admitted, "yes."

"I'm sorry to disappoint you," Roxy said. "But this is all I have to offer you."

"Is this because I lied?" Jane demanded.

"Jane—" Johnny said.

"No Johnny," Jane said, "that's what she wants. She wants to convince you that you can handle Hitch, so you'll face him and he'll kill you. All because I lied."

"I should let you get killed," Roxy said, angrily, "both of you! You lied and used my desire to see my father against me."

"See?" Jane said to Johnny.

"But I'm not going to do that," Roxy said. "I'm offering you my help. It's up to you if you want it or not." She grabbed her beer and stood up. "You can let me know tomorrow."

She walked to the bar with her beer. The men there looked at her but gave her room.

"Somethin' wrong?" the bartender asked.

"No, nothing," she said. "Is this place named after you?"

"Sorry?"

"The Grizzly," she said. "You look kind of like a grizzly bear. You must know that."

"So I've been told." He smiled, and his teeth flashed from behind all the hair, matching the sparkle in his blue eyes.

"So, is it named after you?"

"No," he said. "It's named after an actual grizzly bear, though. The one that mauled me."

"So you own it?"

"I do."

"And you were mauled by a bear?"

"I was."

"And you're alive to talk about it."

"I am," he said. "Sadly, the grizzly who mauled me isn't."

"Who killed it?" she asked.

"I did," he said.

"Wow," she said, "that must be some story."

"It is, he said, "but I can't tell it here. I can only tell it somewhere private."

"Do you have someplace in mind?" she asked.

"I do, yeah," he said, "but you'd have to stick around til closin', or come back."

"For a story like that," she said, "I guess I'll just stick around."

"Good." He put his hand out. "My name's Case."

"Roxy."

"Happy to meet you, Roxy."

As he walked away she thought, not as happy as you're going to be.

***

After a while Johnny and Jane got up and left, presumably to go back to their hotel. Or they might have been mounting up, or hitching up, to leave town. If they wanted to do that, and keep running, that was up to them.

Roxy had no intention of killing a man for them—especially when it sounded like she would have to kill a lot of other men first, to get to Hitch. She had every reason not to do it.

She wasn't even very sure why she had offered to help them at all. That might have been something else she learned from the Gunsmith, helping people in need. Clint Adams could never resist that and, apparently, neither could Roxy Doyle.

Case brought her another beer, smiled, and went off to serve others.

***

At closing time Case locked the door behind the last customer, then turned to face Roxy, who was still at the bar.

"So where is this private place you were talking about?" she asked.

He smiled broadly and said, "You're lookin' at it."

"Right here?"

He walked to her, put his hands on her waist, lifted her up onto the bar and said, "This is as good a place as any."

Chapter Twenty-One

Roxy had never had sex on a bar before.

And she had never been with a man who had this much hair.

But those eyes did something to her, and so did his smile.

And once he had her up on the bar, his hands started doing things to her, as well.

She took the time to remove her gun belt and set it aside within easy reach, but from that point on he undressed her, starting with her boots, then her pants, and shirt, until he had her totally and gloriously naked on the bar.

"You're beautiful," he said, "like a painting. I wish I could put you up on the wall behind this bar."

"Well, you can't," she said. "You've got me naked on your bar. So what do you intend to do with me?"

"I'm gonna do with you, to you," he said, "and for you."

"Well honey," she said, "then I'm all yours."

He ran his hands over her. They were large hands, with thick fingers, and yet his touch was incredibly tender. Her nipples stood out even before he got to them, touched them, stroked them, pinched them, and then leaned forward and licked them with his tongue. He spread her legs out so he could clearly see the red patch of hair between them, but then he stood between her thighs, gathered her in and kissed her. She felt the hair of his beard on her face, but even more she felt his lips. When he started to move them down her body, she spread her legs wider to give him room. He crouched down in front of her and his beard hair mingled with her pubic patch as his tongue probed her.

She scooted forward on the bar so she could close her thighs on his head, and hold him there as his tongue avidly licked her, building her to an explosion of pleasure.

He stood up then, lifted her off the bar, but didn't put her down. Instead, he kissed her deeply, a kiss she avidly returned. This was unlike any experience she had ever had before, and she wanted to keep it going.

"I can't lift you onto the bar," she said, "but I can undress you."

So he put her down and she proceeded to do just that.

***

In their hotel room Johnny and Jane Billings sat on their bed and stared at each other.

"Is this what we wanted?" she asked him.

"This is what Roxy is willin' to give us," he said. "I think we better take it."

"And what do we do when we come face to face with Hitch?" Jane asked.

"I think when that happens," he said, "Roxy won't have much choice but to be who she is, Lady Gunsmith."

"You really think so?"

"She won't just stand there and let me die, Jane," Johnny said.

"What about the money?" Jane asked. "She doesn't think I knew about it."

"That was just the way I wanted to play it," he said. "Let her have a bad opinion about me, not you."

"She already hates me," Jane said. "I lied to her."

"Look, Jane," Johnny said, "our plan worked. We have her just where we want her. Let's not worry about any of that other stuff."

He reached out and pulled her to him, hugged her tightly.

"I told you," he said, "we were gonna have all the money we need, and the place to live that we wanted. I promised, didn't I?"

"Yes, you did," she said. "You promised."

"And I always keep my word, don't I?"

"Yes, you do, Johnny," Jane said. "You do. It's just . . ."

"Just what?"

"What's gonna happen when she realizes what we did?" Jane asked.

"We'll worry about that when the time comes."

***

When Roxy had Case as naked as she was she stood back to take a look. He was built like a tree trunk, powerful thighs and legs holding up a thick body, which sported an equally thick penis. His body was covered with hair, and he really did resemble a grizzly, but at that moment she found it very exciting.

She got to her knees on the dirty saloon floor—the bottom of her bare feet were already black from it—and took his penis in both hands. She fondled it first, then leaned forward and ran her tongue over it. When she had it good and wet and gleaming with her saliva, she opened her mouth and took it in. Case groaned and went up onto his toes as she began to suck him.

She ran her hands up the back of his thighs to cup his strong buttocks and pull him to her as she glided her lips over him, taking him in and out.

"Jesus, woman!" he said, at one point. He reached down and pried her mouth off him, then lifted her up and carried her to a table. He set her down, spread her legs, and poked himself into her, cleaving her easily because she was so wet. From there he proceeded to fuck her brutally, which delighted her. There was no desire in her whatsoever for a tender, gentle fuck. This was meant to be adventurous.

And it was never going to happen again, so she might as well go all out and enjoy every minute of it.

Chapter Twenty-Two

The next morning Roxy woke feeling the effects of the brutal coupling with Case, the bartender. And in bringing it all back to mind, she recalled how much she didn't like men with a lot of hair on their body. All the more reason the session would never be repeated—aside from her usual rule of not sleeping with the same man twice.

So instead of thinking about that, she started planning what kind of regimen she would put Johnny through, to prepare him to face Hitch. She could run him through the same paces Clint Adams had put her through, but she had been a natural with a gun, and all Clint had to do was hone her skill. She had no idea how good or inept Johnny was with a gun, so that was the first thing they were going to have to find out.

She would also need to know the same thing about this fellow Hitch, who she had never heard of before now. Johnny was going to have to tell her all he knew about the man, because she had nobody else to ask. She could send a telegram to Clint Adams to see what he knew, but at the moment she had no idea where he was.

She decided before she dealt with Johnny and Jane, to deal with the way she felt, and that meant soaking in a hot bath.

***

She left the hotel an hour later, feeling much better. She figured Johnny and Jane were still in their room, not wanting to be seen on the streets. She decided instead of stopping in to see them, to find a place where she and Johnny could work on his ability with a gun.

Ideally, if they rode out of town and found a clearing, that would work. But in town there might be an empty lot somewhere—considering Paris was so small and filled with buildings that were deteriorating.

She only had to walk two blocks when she found what she wanted. It looked as if the building that had been there had burned to the ground, recently. The remnants had not been cleared away, but there was enough room for her to erect a small shooting range.

She turned and headed back to the hotel.

***

"I need you," she said, when Johnny opened the door.

"I thought it was us who needed you," Jane said, from her place on the bed.

"I found a space for us to use," Roxy said. "Now we're going to need a bunch of bottles and cans to shoot at."

"Is that gonna help Johnny face Hitch?" Jane asked. "Shooting at a bunch of bottles and cans?"

"It's going to help me see how much work I have to do," Roxy said. "Do you have a gun?"

Johnny walked to the bed, reached under it and came out with a gun belt and gun.

"A Navy Colt?" Roxy said.

"What's wrong with it?"

"It's just not ideal for what we need to do," Roxy said. "I'm afraid you're going to have to use some of your money, Johnny."

"For what?" Jane asked.

"To buy a new gun and holster," Roxy said. "And we better get started."

"We haven't had breakfast, yet," Jane complained.

"And that's a perfect place to start," Roxy told her.

***

They went to Paris' only decent café to have breakfast. While they ate Roxy asked questions. Did Johnny feel more comfortable with a rifle or a pistol? Had he ever shot a man before? Or even faced one with a gun?

Johnny said he felt he was better with a rifle, since he had done some hunting. And no, he had never shot a man, or even faced one with a gun.

"It just ain't happened," he finished.

"At your age," Roxy said, "that's kind of unusual."

"My age?"

"Well, how old are you?" Roxy asked. "Fifty?"

"I'm only forty-four," Johnny said. "I mean, I know I look a little worse than that, but—"

"Well," Roxy said, "even at forty-four you'd think you had to shoot at somebody at least once. In a war?"

"No war," Johnny said.

"In a saloon?" Roxy said. "Some drunk?"

"I can usually talk my way out of a drunken situation like that," Johnny said.

"Johnny's a really good talker," Jane concurred.

"What about you, Jane?"

"I'm thirty-eight," she said. "I know I look older—"

Roxy thought she was lying, that she was in her mid-40s—possibly even older than Johnny—but that didn't matter, at the moment.

"Have you ever fired a gun?" Roxy asked.

"Fired one, yes," Jane said. "Hit anything? No."

"Okay," Roxy said, "so we'll just concentrate on what Johnny can do with a gun."

"So where do we start?" Jane asked.

"Like we said," Roxy answered. "Breakfast first. Then we'll go buy Johnny a gun. After that, we'll set up a shooting range."

"With cans and bottles," Jane said.

"Right."

Jane stood up.

"Then let's get started."

Chapter Twenty-Three

Johnny missed his first six shots.

Didn't even come close.

"Must be this new gun," he complained, looking at the Colt in his hand.

"It's not the gun, Johnny. Okay," Roxy said. "Let's just see how you do with the rifle."

Roxy gave him her rifle.

"Three bottles, three cans," she told him.

"Three bottles, three cans," he repeated, then took aim.

She tried to get him to aim with the rifle, but with the pistol, just point. She and Clint Adams had the same natural ability with a hand gun. Whatever they pointed at, they hit. It was just as if the gun barrel was an extension of their finger.

He fired six times. Two cans leaped in the air, and one bottle shattered.

"Shit!" he swore.

"Take it easy," Jane called out to him from the sidelines.

"Relax," Roxy said. "I'll reload, you go and set up more cans and bottles."

"Okay."

He ran over to the fence they'd erected and set the bottles and cans in place.

"Johnny! Watch!" Roxy shouted.

Johnny turned, and Roxy drew and fired six times in quick succession. Cans flew, bottles shattered and Johnny ducked.

"See?" Roxy called, ejecting the spent shells and loading live ones, "just don't think about it."

"Jesus Christ!" Jane said. "I've never seen anything like that."

Johnny set up six more targets and walked shakily back to stand next to Roxy.

"That was amazin'," he said. "And scary. Do you really think I could ever do that?"

"No," Roxy said, honestly, "but let's see how much improvement we can muster."

They got back to it.

***

Roxy was setting up more targets when she saw a man walking toward them. The sunlight glinted off the badge on his chest.

Roxy approached Johnny and Jane.

"Don't panic," Roxy said. "Here comes a lawman."

"Where?" Johnny turned.

"Do like she says, Johnny," Jane said. "Relax."

The lawman stepped onto the lot and approached them. He was an average height man in his 40s, with a bemused expression.

"Practicing?" he asked.

"Pretty much," Roxy said.

"I got a report there was some shots fired," he said.

People had been stopping by during the morning to watch, and then move on. Maybe one of them had reported the shooting.

"For what?" the sheriff asked. "Is there some kind of contest comin' up I should know about?"

"Not that I know of," Roxy said. "My friend just asked me to help him . . . learn."

"Uh-huh," the lawman said. "Why?"

"Sorry?"

"Why would he, a man, ask you, a woman?" the sheriff asked.

"Do you see something wrong in that?" Roxy asked.

"Well . . . yeah."

"What's your name, Sheriff?"

"Jim Everett," he said. "Sheriff Everett."

"I met your deputy, Andy. He didn't tell you about me?"

"I ain't seen Andy today."

"Haven't you ever seen a woman shoot before?" she asked.

"Well . . . no." The sheriff looked confused.

"Show him, Roxy," Jane suggested.

"No," Roxy said, "that won't solve anything."

"It'll show him that a woman can shoot," Jane said.

"Yeah, Miss . . . Roxy?" Sheriff Everett said. "Why don't you show me?"

"Why don't you show me how you can shoot, Sheriff?" Roxy asked.

"I can shoot better than any woman I ever met," the man said.

"Well," Jane said, "you never met Roxy Doyle."

"Jane!"

"Doyle?" Sheriff Everett said. "Roxy Doyle? Why does that name sound—oh, wait."

Roxy waited, to see what he was going to come up with. She was very close to wanting to show off for him, though not quite yet.

"Wait, I know," he said. "There's supposed to be a Roxy Doyle that people call Lady Gunsmith."

"That's her!" Jane said.

"You're Lady Gunsmith?" Everett asked.

"Yes, she is," Jane said. She couldn't seem to keep her mouth shut. Meanwhile, Johnny just kept quiet.

"You've heard of her," Jane said.

"Yeah, but I thought . . ."

"What?" Roxy asked. "You thought what?"

"I thought it was just, you know, a story. I mean, a woman who can outshoot men? That's not very likely, is it?"

Roxy looked at Jane, who smiled.

Chapter Twenty-Four

Sheriff Jim Everett stepped up, drew his gun and fired six times, very deliberately. Three bottles shattered and two cans flew into the air.

"Not bad," Jane said.

"I barely missed that third can," Everett said, holstering his gun. He looked at Johnny. "You wanna try?"

"No, thanks," Johnny said. "I couldn't do that good."

Everett looked at Roxy.

"Then I guess it's up to you, Lady Gunsmith," he said. "Show me what you can do."

Jane ran over to set up six more bottles and cans, and then got out of the way.

"Now, just take your time—" Everett started, but Roxy drew and fired six times even faster than she had before. Bottles and cans danced and fell to the ground.

She turned to the sheriff, reloading before holstering her weapon.

"Anything else I can do for you?" she asked.

His eyes were wide, but then he narrowed them, trying to hide his surprise.

"Uh, I actually came over to tell you to take this outside the town limits," he said.

"Of course," she said. "we can do that."

"And do you have any idea how long you'll be in town?" he asked.

"Probably a couple of more days," she said.

"Well," the sheriff said, "if you are the Lady Gunsmith, I'd appreciate having no trouble while you're here."

"I'll do my best," she said.

"Right," he said. "Okay, so . . . outside of town."

"Got it," Roxy said.

The sheriff nodded, turned and walked away. She had a feeling Deputy Andy was going to get a talking to for not telling the sheriff she was in town.

Jane came running up to Roxy, gleefully.

"Did you see his face?" she asked, "'A woman who can outshoot me?' Omigod!" She laughed.

"What are we gonna do now?" Johnny asked.

"Well, like the sheriff said," Roxy replied, "we'll go find a new spot outside of town."

"How do we get the bottles and cans out there?" Jane asked.

"We'll rent a buckboard," Roxy said. "Come on, let's get it done."

***

Sheriff Jim Everett stopped in both of Paris' saloons to pass the word that the Lady Gunsmith was in town. That was because he was so shocked there really was a Lady Gunsmith, and that she could shoot as well as she did. And this was the kind of thing that a big mouth like Jim Everett could not keep to himself.

***

In the second saloon, the Wagon Wheel, four men sat in the back and listened to Sheriff Everett tell his tale.

"You should've seen her shoot," he was telling the bartender. "A woman! It's crazy that a woman can shoot like that."

The bartender agreed and gave the sheriff another drink.

"Whataya think?" Monte George asked his partners.

"About what?" Dumb Donnie asked.

"Not talkin' to you, Donnie."

Donnie shrugged, went back to thinking about whatever it was he wasn't thinking about.

"Trace?" Monte said.

"The sheriff's got a big mouth, Monte."

"Yeah, but he don't lie," Monte said. "If the Lady Gunsmith is in town, then we should get Donnie in front of her."

"What?" Dumb Donnie asked.

"Still not talkin' to you, Donnie," Monte said.

"Oh."

"You think Donnie can outdraw Lady Gunsmith?" Woody asked.

"Dumb Donnie is the fastest gun in the county," Monte said. "Whatayou think?"

"How do we get her to do it?" Woody asked.

"Well," Monte said, "Everett is sayin' that they're outside of town, shootin' at targets."

"So?" Trace asked.

"So here's what we do," Monte said.

***

Outside of town they stopped the buckboard in a clearing that looked like a good place to set up. They brought some wood along to build a fence, but instead found a fallen tree that was large enough to hold the target bottles and cans. Once they had them set up they got started with the lessons again.

"Okay," Roxy said, "now remember what I told you. Point, don't aim, and squeeze the trigger, don't jerk it."

"I remember," Johnny said, adjusting the holster on his hip.

Jane stood off to one side, arms folded, and Roxy said, "All right, go ahead."

When the first shot rang out Roxy noticed that Johnny had not yet drawn his gun.

When the second shot sounded she yelled, "Take cover!"

PART TWO

Chapter Twenty-Five

"What the hell?" Johnny shouted, from behind a rock.

The firing continued for a few more volleys, and then stopped.

"What do we do now?" Jane asked from behind the buckboard.

"We find out who they are and what they want," Roxy answered from her place behind a nearby tree.

"How do we do that?"

"We ask them."

Johnny and Jane fell silent.

"Hello out there!" Roxy shouted.

"That you? Lady Gunsmith?"

"It's me," she replied. "What do you want?"

"What do ya think?"

"Well," she called back, "if you want what I think you do, then you want to die."

She heard laughter, counted three or four different men.

"Come on, now," she called. "How many are you, and who's first?"

"Why don't you step out and see?" the man called back.

"So you can gun me down from hiding?" Roxy asked. "That'll sure give you a big reputation."

"We got a fella here who can beat you fair," the man said, "just you and him."

"Then have him step out," Roxy said, "and let's see where it goes from there."

After a few moments of silence, the man said, "Just you and him?"

"That's right."

"Do we got your word you won't shoot 'im as soon as he shows himself?"

"You do. And do I have your word that you won't all shoot me when I show myself?"

"You got it."

Even so, Roxy had no way of knowing what they would do after she gunned the man down.

"Okay, then," she called.

"Roxy," Jane hissed, "you really think they're gonna keep their word?"

"There's only one way to find out, Jane."

"Do you want us to step out with you?" Jane asked.

"What?" Johnny said, nervously. "No, she, uh, gave her word she'd do it alone."

"He's right," Roxy said. "He'd just get killed. So would you."

"And what if you get killed?" Jane asked.

"I won't," Roxy said, "but if I do. Run."

Roxy stood up and stepped out into the open, expecting a shot. It didn't come.

A man appeared about thirty feet from her, staggering as if he had been pushed out into the open. He looked back, then turned toward Roxy and wiped his hands on his thighs. He then walked toward Roxy, who also started walking. They stopped when they were about ten feet apart.

"Uh, I'm Donnie," he said.

"Donnie what?"

"They just call me Dumb Donnie."

"Who does?"

"My friends."

"Your friends call you that?" Roxy asked. "They don't sound like very good friends."

"They're the only ones I got," Donnie said. He looked almost 30, but had the mannerisms of a little boy, shrugging and squinting when he spoke, shifting from foot to foot. "Nobody else'll have nothin' to do with me."

"And these are the same friends who just pushed you out here to face me?"

"Uh-huh."

"Why?"

"Because I'm faster'n any of 'em."

"No, Donnie," Roxy said, "I mean why do you let them treat you that way?"

He shrugged.

"They're my friends."

"Friends don't treat each other that way, Donnie," she said. "Not real friends."

"Go on, Donnie!" someone yelled. "Draw on 'er!"

"They want you to draw on me while they hide," Roxy said to him. "They sound like a bunch of cowards."

He laughed at that and said, "Yeah, they do."

"Why don't you tell them to come out here and face me themselves," she suggested. "How many of them are there?"

"Um there's three of 'em," he said. "Uh, I mean, four of us."

"Well, I'm only interested in the three of them, Donnie," Roxy said. "What are their names?"

"There's Monte, Woody and Trace."

"Tell them to step out."

"Um . . ." He raised his eyes to the sky as he called out, "Hey fellas, she, uh, wants you to step out?"

"Come on Monte, Trace, Woody," Roxy shouted. "Don't leave Donnie out here alone."

Donnie and Roxy stood there and waited for an answer.

Chapter Twenty-Six

"Step out," Monte told Trace and Woody.

"What?" Woody asked.

"Out," Monte commanded. "Step out where she can see you."

"W-what if she shoots us?" Trace asked.

"She won't."

"So then you step out," Trace said.

"Look," Monte said, "Dumb Donnie's out there by himself. Are you tellin' me he's braver than you two?"

"No," Woody said, "he's dumber than we are. You want us to step out so you can see if she shoots us."

"That's . . . ridiculous."

"Then you step out," Trace said again. "We'll follow you."

"Jesus—fine!"

Monte George stepped out into the open.

***

Donnie was looking over his shoulder when Monte stepped out.

"That's Monte," he said to Roxy.

"Good to know."

Another man appeared, and then another. They both looked apprehensive.

Monte was handsome, Roxy noticed. On the other hand, the other two were definitely not.

“That’s Woody, and Trace,” Donnie said. “They’re brothers.”

“I can tell.”

“Yeah,” Donnie said, smiling. “They’re kinda funny lookin’.”

“So now what?” Monte asked.

“Now you, Trace, Woody and Donnie go away,” Roxy said. “We’re in the middle of something, here.”

“But what are ya doin’?” Monte asked. “A shootin’ match? Let Donnie shoot.”

“Why?” Roxy asked.

Monte started walking toward them, followed by the two brothers.

“Because he’s good,” Monte said. “He’s real good. Maybe better than you.”

“Monte,” she said, “I need you and your two friends to do something for me.”

“What?”

“Drop your guns. Then we can keep talking.”

“Sure,” Monte said. “Do it, boys.”

All three of them removed their revolver from their belt and dropped them to the ground. Donnie was the only one wearing a holster.

"Now we can talk," Roxy said. "What is it you fellas want, exactly?"

"We want Donnie to shoot it out with you," Monte said.

"Who, wait—" Donnie said.

"You mean face-to-face?" Roxy asked. "To the death."

"Huh? Wait—" Donnie said.

"No," Monte said, "Donnie ain't never shot it out with anybody that way. No, no, just targets, like you're doin' here with this fella."

"I'm teaching this man," Roxy said, "not playing with him."

"Donnie can shoot better than any man we know," Monte said. "And better than any woman, including you."

She studied all four men. They were the same age, late-20s', probably grew up together. Donnie had looked apprehensive for a moment, but now just stared blankly at her.

"I'll do it on one condition," she said, finally.

"What's that?" Monte asked.

"You have to stop calling him Dumb Donnie."

"If you win," Monte said.

"No," she said, "if I do it at all, no matter who wins."

"But we gotta be shootin' for somethin'," Monte said.

"I think bragging rights would be good enough for you," Roxy said.

"And what about you?" Monte asked.

"Oh, if I win," she said, "I'm not going to be bragging about it to anyone. I'm just doing it so my student, here, can watch."

"This ol' guy can't shoot?" Monte asked.

"Hey—" Johnny said, speaking for the first time.

"Forget it, Johnny," Roxy said, cutting him off. "Can you shoot, Monte?"

"I can shoot, but not as good as Donnie."

"So Donnie's going to do the shooting for you."

"Well, yeah."

"Then shut up about Johnny," she said. "Now pick your guns up out of the dirt and unload them. Then put them back in your belts."

They did as she told them.

"I'll shoot the first man who tries to load his gun. Got it?" she asked.

"We got it," Monte said.

She looked at Donnie.

"You sure you want to do this?"

Donnie shrugged.

"Monte says I gotta."

"Do you always do what Monte tells you to do?" she asked.

"Well, sure."

And she could tell that he didn't see any reason why he shouldn't.

Chapter Twenty-Seven

Johnny set up the targets, while Monte, Trace and Woody stood off to one side.

"Go on, Donnie!" Monte yelled. "Shoot. Show 'er."

But Donnie looked at Roxy.

"A lady should go first, Miss," he said.

"That's okay, Donnie," she said. "Your friends are very anxious to see you shoot."

"If you say so, Miss."

"And just call me Roxy."

"Yes, Miss."

Donnie turned to face the target bottles and cans.

"Fast or slow, Miss?" he asked.

"Just hit as many of them as you can, Donnie."

"Yes, Miss."

Donnie drew his gun deliberately and fired 6 shots. 4 bottles shattered and 2 cans leaped into the air.

"There ya go!" Monte shouted, and his three friends cheered.

"Very impressive, Donnie."

"Thank you, Miss."

She noticed he holstered his gun without ejecting the spent shells and replacing them with live rounds. He certainly wasn't worried about being caught with an empty gun.

"Beat that, lady," Monte called.

Johnny ran over to set up 6 more targets, 3 bottles and 3 cans.

Roxy stepped, drew, fired 6 times, hitting all 6 targets.

"That was really good, Miss," Donnie said.

"Thank you, Donnie."

"You beat 'er, Donnie," Monte yelled out.

"I don't think so," Johnny spoke up. "I think Roxy won."

"Set the targets up again!" Monte called out. "They should shoot at the same time."

Donnie looked at Roxy.

"Fast, this time?" he asked.

"Fast," she said, with a nod.

Johnny got 12 targets set up, this time, 6 bottles, 6 cans.

"Three bottles, three cans each," Roxy said.

"Right," Donnie said.

"Johnny, you call it," Roxy said.

"On three," Johnny said, while Jane stood off to the side. "One . . . two . . . three!"

Roxy and Donnie drew. Roxy was shocked at Donnie's speed, but knew she had beat him by a good second or two.

"Donnie wins!" Monte shouted.

"No," Johnny said, "it was Roxy."

"You're a liar!"

"He is not!" Jane shouted.

"I've got an idea," Roxy said. "Donnie can shoot all cans, I'll shoot all bottles. That way we should be able to tell who finishes first." She looked at Donnie. "Okay with you?"

"Fine with me," he said, with a shrug. She had the feeling it didn't matter to him who was faster, but it also didn't occur to him not to try his hardest.

"Stand side-by-side," Johnny said, "but make sure you have room to draw."

Roxy and Donnie lined up next to each other, then made sure they were a couple of arm lengths apart.

"On three," Johnny said. "One . . . two . . . three!"

There was a cacophony of shots. Bottles exploded, cans flew into the air.

And one bottle stood alone.

"Roxy wins!" Johnny shouted. "He missed one."

"Damn it!" Monte swore. "Dumb Donnie—"

"You can't call him that anymore," Roxy said, "remember?"

"Yeah, yeah . . ."

"I don't have time for you, anymore," Roxy said. "You and your friends better get back to town."

"You're good," Monte said. "I'll give you that."

"I'm not flattered," she said. "And don't any of you reload your guns until you get back to town."

"Yeah, okay," Monte said.

"Except you, Donnie," she said. "Reload now and do it after every time you shoot. Understand?"

"I understand," Donnie said, reloading his gun. "Thanks, Roxy."

Monte and the others started back to where they had left their horses. As Donnie turned to follow, Roxy grabbed his arm.

"You don't have to stay with them, you know," she said.

"Why not?"

"They're not really your friends."

He frowned, looking puzzled.

"But . . . I don't have any other friends."

"You have."

"Are we friends?"

"Yes, we are."

He smiled.

"I like that," he said. "I don't have any lady friends. But . . ." He looked after the others, who had disappeared from sight. "I have to go."

"Why?" she asked.

"They have my horse."

Now she smiled.

"Okay, Donnie," she said. "But remember, we're friends, now."

"Yeah," he said, "we're friends."

He trotted off after his other friends.

Roxy turned to Johnny and Jane and said, "Let's get back to it."

Chapter Twenty-Eight

"She's a bitch!" Monte said.

They were back in town, at a table in the Wagon Wheel Saloon.

"She was good," Trace said.

"She was lucky!" Monte argued.

"Once is lucky," Woody said.

"Shut up," Monte said. "She's a bitch, and she's gonna get hers."

"That ain't nice."

Monte, Woody and Trace looked at Donnie, who didn't look happy.

"What?" Monte asked.

"I said that ain't nice," Donnie said.

"Whatta you know, Dumb Donnie?" Monte asked.

"And you ain't supposed to call me that no more," Donnie said. "You told Roxy—"

"Roxy?" Monte said. "You call her Roxy? Is she your girlfriend now?"

"She's my friend," Donnie said. "That's all."

"She ain't your friend," Monte said. "We're your friends. Don't forget that."

"Not if you're plannin' on hurtin' Roxy," Donnie said.

Monte laughed, looked at Trace and Woody, who weren't sure what was going on.

"And who's gonna stop us, Donnie?" Monte asked.

Donnie stood up from the table and said, "Me, Monte. I'm gonna stop you."

Donnie's stance made Monte think he was ready to go for his gun, and Monte knew he couldn't go up against Dumb Donnie that way.

"Whoa, Donnie whoa," Monte said. "Take it easy."

"You ain't gonna hurt Roxy," Donnie said.

"You're right," Monte said. "We ain't gonna hurt her."

Donnie looked at Trace and Woody, and they both nodded their agreement, keeping their hands above the table so Donnie could see them.

"It's okay, buddy," Monte said, "it's okay. Settle down. Have a drink with us."

Donnie looked at the three of them, then eased his stance and sat back down.

"That's better," Monte said, slapping Donnie on the back. "Woody, get us some beers,"

"Right, right," Woody said, getting up and going to the bar.

When he returned, he laid out the four mugs of beer and sat back down.

"There ya go, buddy," Monte said to Donnie. "You did good today, you know that?"

"Thanks, Monte."

"You did real good." Monte patted him on the back again. "Real good. Drink up."

***

"We're done for today," Roxy said.

"Are you sure?" Jane asked.

Roxy smiled.

"We're out of targets," she said. "We used some up with Donnie."

"You were great," Jane said. She looked over at Johnny, who was staring off into space with his hand on his gun. "What's he doin'?"

"He's seeing it in his head," Roxy said.

"Is that what you do?" Jane asked. "See it in your head?"

"No," Roxy said. "It's different for me."

"Why?" Jane asked. "How?"

"I feel it," Roxy said. "I know it. Each time I shoot I know I'm going to hit what I'm shooting at."

"But . . . how?"

"It just comes natural."

"And you can't teach that to Johnny?"

"It can't be taught," Roxy said. "But I had somebody recognize it in me, and he helped me recognize it, and use it."

"Can you do somethin' like that for Johnny?"

"I can try," Roxy said. "I can probably get him to be as good with a gun as he can be."

"But will that be good enough?" Jane asked. "Good enough to handle Hitch?"

"That's what we're going to find out."

***

They went back to town, but before getting some supper, Johnny and Jane went back to their hotel room.

Roxy arranged to meet them at a café down the street from the hotel. After she was seated and a waitress brought her a cup of coffee, she thought about her father.

What she was doing was not getting her any closer to Gavin Doyle. On the other hand, she had no clue about where her father was at the moment, not even any rumors to follow. So here she was involved in somebody else's business, something the Gunsmith warned her about, but usually ended up doing himself.

Which didn't make it a good idea.

Chapter Twenty-Nine

She was too easy a mark.

That was what Roxy was thinking, now. By letting Jane lie to her, lead her on a merry chase, and then agreeing to help her and her husband anyway, she had made herself an easy mark. Perhaps she was better off leaving Paris and leaving them to their own devices. She decided to discuss it with them at supper.

***

"Donnie ain't gonna like this," Woody said.

"I don't care," Monte said. "I want her dead."

"Whataya gonna tell him?" Trace asked.

"That she started it," Monte said, "and we finished it."

"Are we gonna follow her?" Woody asked.

"No," Monte said, "we're just gonna wait."

***

"You want to what?" Jane asked.

"Get back to what I was doing," Roxy repeated, "looking for my father."

"But you can't," Jane said. "We haven't finished—"

"I have," she said, cutting her off. "In fact, I never should have started. This isn't any of my business."

"But you can't—"

"Stop, Jane," Johnny said.

"But Johnny, she can't—"

"Yeah, she can," Johnny said, cutting into his steak. "We lied to her, and she's been nice enough to help us anyway."

"But she hasn't helped enough!" Jane argued. "You can't face Hitch."

"I'll just have to," Johnny said. "It's my problem, not yours, and not hers."

Jane gave Roxy a hard look.

"Don't try that on me, Jane," Roxy said.

"Try what?"

"To make my feel guilty," Roxy said. "I have nothing to feel guilty about."

"And I have?"

Roxy didn't respond.

"Well, I don't feel guilty," Jane said. "I told you from the start—"

"—yes, I know," Roxy said. "You were desperate."

"I still am!" Jane said. "I'm not gonna let Johnny go up against Hitch alone and get himself killed."

"So you'll go with him?" Roxy asked. "And get yourself killed with him?"

"If I have to!"

"No, you won't," Johnny said. "Now just keep quiet and eat."

They finished their meal in silence, then paid their check and left the café. Jane walked off a few feet and stood, arms folded, fuming.

"Don't mind her," Johnny said. "I don't blame you for bein' done with us. When will you be leavin' town?"

"Tomorrow," she said.

"Early?"

"Not too early," she answered. "There's no rush."

"Well," Johnny said, "thanks for your help, up to now."

"You're welcome," she said.

"And don't feel guilty," he said, "no matter what you hear."

"Don't worry," she said. "I won't."

Johnny walked over to Jane, put his arms around her and walked away. He was wearing his gun. At least he had learned that much.

***

As Johnny and Jane entered the hotel lobby, he suddenly stopped.

"What's wrong?" she asked.

"I saw somebody across the street."

"Hitch?" she asked, fearfully.

"No," Johnny said, "but somebody I recognize."

"From where?"

"From here," he said. "You better go upstairs."

"But Johnny—"

"Go," he said, "now!"

She ran up the steps. He turned and looked out the front window.

***

Roxy considered getting a drink but didn't want to chance running into Donnie and his friends. So instead she simply walked a while, convincing herself she was doing the right thing, and then headed back to her hotel.

***

"Here she comes," Monte said, as Roxy Doyle came walking up the street.

"Whatta we do?" Woody asked.

"Just start shootin' when I do," Monte said.

Chapter Thirty

As Roxy approached the hotel, she saw Johnny looking out the window from the lobby. He was either watching somebody or waiting for her. Maybe he wanted to talk to her without his wife around.

As she stepped up onto the boardwalk to enter the hotel, she heard something behind her, and then Johnny shouted, “Look out!” as he broke the glass.

Turning, she saw Monte, Woody and Trace across the street, all brandishing their guns. As they started to fire, she drew and heard shots from behind her.

The street in front of the hotel was deserted at that hour, most businesses having already closed. The three men charged her as they fired. She stood her ground, drew and fired coolly.

***

Johnny saw the men firing at Roxy as she calmly drew her gun to fire back. He was amazed at how still she was. But he knew there was always the chance that a bullet could hit her. So he began to fire.

He pulled the trigger until the hammer fell on empty chambers. The sound of the shots were deafening, and he would not find out until later if he even hit any of the shooters. But, at the very least, he had given her some warning.

***

Her first shot hit Monte in the chest, driving him back a few feet with a shocked look on his face before he fell over onto his back.

Woody was next, the bullet striking just below his Adam's apple. His body fell to the ground like a marionette whose strings had been cut.

Finally, poor Trace was struck by two bullets, one from her gun, and one from Johnny's, who had been firing from the window.

With all three men on the ground, Roxy turned to look at Johnny who was still in the window. The look on his face was one of pure shock, either at what had happened, or at what he had done.

***

By the time the shooting stopped, a small crowd had gathered on both sides of the street and the sheriff appeared.

"What the hell—" Sheriff Everett shouted. "What'd you do, woman?"

"I defended myself," she said. "They charged at me from across the street like madmen."

"The three of them?"

"That's right."

"How many times did you fire?"

"Three?"

"Three shots, three dead men?"

"I try to conserve my ammunition."

The sheriff examined the three men, then stood up and looked at Roxy.

"This one was shot twice."

"That was me," a man's voice said. Johnny came out the front door of the hotel and stood next to Roxy.

"You shot this man?" the lawman asked.

"Yes," Johnny said, "from the window. I saw the three of them waitin' across the street and felt like they was up to somethin'."

"And they were."

"Yeah," Johnny said, "they tried to kill Roxy."

"And I defended myself," Roxy said, again, "with Johnny's help."

At that moment Jane came running from the hotel. She rushed to her husband.

"Johnny! Are you all right?"

"I'm fine," he said.

"I'll need you both to come to my office," Everett said. "I'll need statements, since you both killed somebody."

"No problem, Sheriff," Roxy said. "We'll be there."

Everett turned and started shouting for volunteers to remove the bodies from the street. Roxy turned to Johnny and Jane.

"How did you know?" Roxy asked Johnny.

"I saw them across the street when we got back," he said. "I thought they might be up to somethin'. I figured I'd stay in the lobby and watch."

"He made me go upstairs," Jane said, "and then he saved your life."

"Well," Johnny replied, "I wouldn't say that."

"Why not?" Jane asked. "You killed them didn't you?"

"I shot one of them," he said. "But I'm sure Roxy killed all three herself."

"How can you be sure?" Jane asked.

"I may have hit one of them once," Johnny said, "but I fired six shots."

Chapter Thirty-One

In the sheriff's office they each made a statement and signed it.

"I was planning on leaving town tomorrow, Sheriff," Roxy said. "Any reason why I can't?"

"No," Everett said, "your stories match."

"So they can leave, too?" Roxy asked, indicating Johnny and Jane.

"Sure, why not? Just do me a favor, will you?"

"What's that?" Roxy asked.

"Stay out of trouble before you go."

"That's my plan," she said. She looked at the couple. "Let's go."

***

Roxy invited them both to the Wagon Wheel Saloon.

"Why should we go with you?" Jane asked. "After what you said to us?"

"Because we have to talk," Roxy said.

"About what?" Jane asked.

"About what I said to you."

"Let's have a drink, Jane," Johnny said. "What can it hurt?"

***

They went to the Wagon Wheel, where Roxy bought three beers and they settled down at a back table.

"I thought you were done with us?" Jane said to her.

"That was before," Roxy said.

"Before what?"

"You were right when you said Johnny saved my life," Roxy said.

"Who are you kiddin'?" Johnny asked. "You killed those three easy as you please."

"But only because of your warning," Roxy told him.

"I still think you woulda killed 'em," Johnny said. "You were turnin' even before I broke the window."

"That may be," Roxy said, "but I feel I owe you, now."

"So you're back with us?" Jane asked.

Roxy had thought it over very quickly. It was unclear whether or not Johnny had actually saved her life, but he had at least tried to. That was enough to make her feel beholding to him.

"Yes," she said, "I'm back with you."

"But you told the sheriff you're leaving town tomorrow," Jane said.

"I am and so are you two."

"Where are we going?" Jane asked.

"That's for you to tell me," Roxy said. "Where do we find Hitch Moran?"

***

Roxy was in her hotel room, packing her saddlebags, when there was a knock at the door. When she opened it she saw Donnie standing there.

"You killed Monte and the others," he said.

"Come on in, Donnie," she said. "I'll explain."

He entered, but said, "You don't gotta. I heard about it, already. They tried ta kill you."

"Yes, they did."

"I'm glad they didn't," he said. "They lied to me. We had a fight, and they swore they wasn't gonna hurt you. If they killed you, I woulda killed them."

"That's sweet, Donnie," she said. He was a handsome young man, so she decided to kiss his cheek. Clumsily, he leaned in, so that their bodies came into contact. She felt the bulge in his pants.

After a shooting Roxy usually experienced the need to feel alive. She often grabbed a man in a saloon, fucked him and discarded him. This time it seemed the man had come to her.

She slid her hand down and felt the bulge through his pants.

"Roxy, Whataya—"

"Shh," she said. "Relax, Donnie. Let me take care of you."

But, as she undid his gunbelt, set it aside, and then unbuttoned his pants, she was actually taking care of herself. And she was going to make sure that he enjoyed it, too.

"I—I ain't done this a lot," he stammered.

"Why not?" she asked. "You're a good-looking boy."

"I don't know ho—oooh, geez," he said, as she freed his cock from the restraint of his pants and underwear, which were now down around his ankles.

She held his hard cock in her hands. She admired both the length and girth of it, then pressed it against her cheek so she could feel the smoothness and heat of it.

"Donnie, this is very pretty."

"Aw, I ain't—oooh."

She cut him off again, this time by licking the length of him.

"This is going to be good, Donnie," she said, standing. She took hold of his cock again and pulled, leading him to the bed. "This is going to be real good."

Chapter Thirty-Two

Roxy removed the rest of Donnie's clothes and laid him down on the bed, on his back. His cock stood straight up, impressively.

Next she took off her own clothes, showing Donnie her beautiful big breasts, lovely freckled skin and the almost burnt orange patch of hair between her legs.

"Oh my God," he said. "I been with whores, but I ain't never seen anybody as beautiful as you."

She smiled.

"You're being sweet again," she said. "Now you're going to get what you deserve."

She got onto the bed with him, pressed her hot flesh against his, and kissed him. He mashed his mouth against hers, urgently.

"Easy," she said, "relax. Let your lips do the work."

This time when they kissed it was better, softer. If he had learned everything he knew about sex from whores, she was going to have to reeducate him.

"Okay, now just relax," she said, sliding her mouth from his. She kissed his neck and shoulders, then moved to his chest, teasing his nipples with her tongue. He tried to put his hands on her, but she swatted them away. "Lie still, hands at your sides."

"Yes, Ma'am."

She continued to kiss her way down his body, pausing at his belly button to tickle it with the point of her tongue. Finally, she was down between his thighs, licking his cock before taking it into her hot mouth.

"Ahhhhh, yesssssss," Donnie said, raising his butt off the bed.

She began to suck him, her head bobbing up and down as his hips moved in unison with her. She enjoyed the way his cock slid in and out of her wet mouth, and the sounds he was making as he neared his explosion. But she stopped before that happened . . .

"Jesus," he begged, "don't stop."

"I'm not stopping," she promised, "just changing position."

She slid up on him until the head of his cock was pressed against her wet pussy lips, and then took him inside, inch by inch.

"Oh God," he said, "you're so . . . hot . . . like a fire . . ."

"And you've got the log to keep it going, handsome," she told him, and started bouncing up and down on him.

She grabbed his hands—which he had obediently been keeping at his sides—and brought them up to her bouncing breasts. Encouraged, he gripped them, squeezed them, rubbed the nipples while she continued to ride him, eyes closed, hoping he would last long enough for her to get where she was going.

Donnie was a young man, and even though he was excited, she could see he was gritting his teeth, trying to last for her—or for himself. He was fighting the urge to explode, but finally she felt it bubble up from inside him, so she hopped off quickly just as he ejaculated. It was like a geyser, hitting the ceiling first, and then across the sheets and off the bed.

"Wow," Roxy said, slapping his belly, "that was a lot."

"It's been a while," he said, shyly.

"I thought you said you've been to whores?"

"Once or twice," he said, "but not for a while."

She laid down next to him, where it was still dry, reached over and took hold of him, again.

"Oh, geez," he said, because he started to get hard again.

"Look at that," she said.

They both watched as he grew in her hand, until he was fully erect.

"Well," she said, getting to her knees and leaning over him, "let's not let this go to waste . . ."

She sucked and rode him again, twice, before finally getting what she wanted, the kind of release that drained all the stress out of her.

He had served his purpose by mostly just lying there. He was too inexperienced to do anything else, and she was kind of tired of teaching men what to do.

She watched him get dressed. As he got older—and maybe a little smarter—she thought he was going to be a heart-breaker.

Fully dressed, he turned and looked at her. She was lying on the bed, still naked. She knew just by looking at him that he was hard again.

"What do I do now?" he asked. "I got no friends."

"You've got me."

"You're leavin' town." Suddenly, an idea occurred to him. "Can I come with you?"

"No," she said, quickly. He was a nice boy, but she didn't need him trailing along after her. He was okay with a gun, but right now his only other talent was getting hard at a moment's notice. There were plenty of other men out there who could do the same.

"You have to stay here, Donnie," she said. "Make new friends."

"Yeah," he said, "yeah, okay. Thanks, Roxy, for, uh, everything."

She smiled at him and said, "Thank *you*."

Chapter Thirty-Three

Roxy met Johnny and Jane in the lobby of the hotel the next morning. They checked out, paying their bills, then went for breakfast.

"Where do we go from here?" Jane asked, over bacon-and-eggs. Roxy had told them to eat well because they would be travelling light for the next few days. Johnny ordered flapjacks and bacon.

"I told you last night, that's up to you," she answered. "Where do we find Hitch?"

"Like we said," Johnny answered, "he's probably in Flagstaff."

"Then we'll head for Flagstaff."

"And get Johnny killed?" Jane demanded. "We should be getting as far from Flagstaff as possible."

"We're not heading there directly," Roxy said. "We've still got some practicing to do."

"But Johnny did good yesterday, right?" Jane asked. "He saved your life."

"Johnny did fine yesterday," Roxy said. "But he did fire six times and only hit someone once."

"But," he said, "in my defense, it was the first time I'd ever fired at a man."

"That's a good point," Roxy agreed, nodding, "but on the other side, now you've gotten the first one out of the way."

"Did I kill him?" Johnny asked. "Or did you?"

"I think we can both take credit for that one," she answered.

***

After breakfast they left the cafe, went to the livery for their horses, then over to the mercantile for just a few supplies: coffee, beef jerky, beans, a coffee pot and a frying pan. They got it all into one gunny sack, then went outside and mounted up. Roxy tied the sack to her saddlehorn before mounting.

As they turned their horses to ride out of town Roxy saw Sheriff Everett watching them from across the street. When he saw that she had noticed him, he tipped his hat.

She ignored him.

***

They rode for half a day before stopping.

"While the horses rest," Roxy said, dismounting, "let's get some shooting in."

"We don't have any targets," Jane pointed out. "No bottles or cans."

"We'll make do with what we have," Roxy said.

"Like what?" Johnny asked.

"Tie the horses off first," Roxy told him, handing him her reins.

While he did that, she found a likely tree with enough branches to use as targets.

"What are you looking at?" Jane asked, coming up alongside her.

"That tree," Roxy said, pointing straight ahead. "That's our target."

"What part? The trunk?"

"The tree trunk *is* as thick as a man," Roxy said. "But those branches on the left, they're as thick as a man's arm. We'll try those first."

Johnny came walking over.

"I'm ready."

"Good," Roxy said. "That tree, see the limbs on the left side?"

Johnny squinted.

"They look like a man's arm," he said.

"That's exactly right," Jane said, anxious to encourage him.

"I want you to hit them," Roxy said.

"How many times?" he asked.

"Well," she said, "let's start with once, and work our way up from there."

"Should I draw and fire?"

"First try hitting what you shoot at," she said, "and then we'll work on your speed."

"Okay," he said, wiping his hands on his thighs, "Here goes."

He fired six shots, very deliberately.

"That was a little better," Roxy admitted. "You hit two."

"It's a little different when nobody's firing back at you," Jane said, giving her husband excuses.

"They weren't shootin' at me," he said. "They was shootin' at Roxy."

"Still . . ." Jane said.

"Reload and try again," Roxy said, "and then we'll move on."

Johnny reloaded his gun, took a stance, and fired six shots.

"He hit it three times!" Jane said. "Right in the trunk."

"Yes," Roxy said, "but he was supposed to hit the tree limbs."

"Shit!" Johnny said.

They remounted and started off.

Chapter Thirty-Four

They rode south for 600 miles, stopping to camp and shoot. Once they stopped for more supplies, although they still kept it to a minimum.

Riding through Utah territory was not comfortable for Roxy. At one point they came within 50 miles of where her father had left her with those people.

Finally, when they crossed the border into Arizona, she began to breathe more easily.

But when they were in Arizona, it was Johnny and Jane who could not breathe easily.

"I'm not gettin' any better, am I?" Johnny asked the day they crossed and camped.

"No," Roxy said.

"So what do we do now?" Jane asked looking across the fire at Roxy. "We'll be in Tuba City tomorrow. From there Hitch might hear that we're there and come after us."

"Me," Johnny said. "He'll come after me."

"I'll be with you," Jane said. "If he comes for you, he comes for me."

Johnny looked at Roxy.

"What do you think?"

"I have an idea," she said, "but I need to work it out. By the time we get to Tuba City, I should be ready to talk about it."

"And what about now?" Johnny said.

"Now," Roxy said, "let's have some more coffee."

***

Late the next afternoon they rode into Tuba City, Arizona. It looked to Roxy like a growing town, many businesses lining the main street, most of them closed now.

"What first?" Jane asked.

"Hotel rooms," Roxy said, "A bath, and then a meal."

"And then you'll tell us your idea?" Johnny asked.

"Yes," Roxy said, "over a steak."

"Sounds good," Johnny said.

***

They found a steakhouse down the street from their hotel. They met there after they had all checked in and had baths.

Johnny and Jane got there first, and as Roxy entered she saw them sitting with their heads together, having a heated conversation.

"Something I should know about?" she asked, taking a seat.

"What?" Jane asked, as they both sat up straight.

"You looked like you were arguing."

"No, not really," Johnny said. "Jane's just . . . worried."

"Are you ready to tell us your idea?" Jane asked.

"Let's order, and then I will," Roxy said, waving at a waiter.

They ordered three steak dinners and then Roxy got down to it.

"I want to ride into Flagstaff alone," Roxy said while they waited.

Johnny and Jane exchanged a look.

"You said you wouldn't face him for me," Johnny reminded her.

"I know," she said, "but that was before you stuck your neck out for me. Besides, I'm not planning to face him, just talk to him."

"You think you can do that?" Johnny asked. "Talk him out of wanting to kill me?"

"I can do that," Roxy said, "if I give him the money back."

Now Johnny and Jane looked at each other again.

"That's never been part of the bargain," Johnny said, finally.

"You don't want to give the money back?"

"If I wanted to do that, I never woulda took it in the first place," Johnny pointed out.

Roxy looked at Jane.

"What about you?"

"It's up to Johnny," Jane said. "I never try to tell him what to do."

"Like stealing the money in the first place, you mean?" Roxy asked.

"I didn't know anything about that," Jane said.

The waiter came over with their steaming plates at that moment.

"Anything else?" he asked.

"No," Roxy said, "we're fine."

The middle-aged waiter looked disappointed at not being able to do something else for the beautiful redhead.

"Now look, Roxy," Johnny said, "that money's all I've got to—"

"Let's eat our suppers," Roxy suggested, "and talk about this later."

"Suits me," Jane said.

Johnny looked dubious, but moments later they were all cutting into their steaks.

Chapter Thirty-Five

After their supper they went across the street to a saloon called—for some reason—The Silver Feather. The place was fairly busy, but they were able to find a table where Roxy could keep her back to a wall.

They sat with three beers and Roxy said, "I'd have an easier time if I was able to give Hitch back the money."

"I've been runnin' with this money a long time, Roxy," Johnny said. "If I give it back, it's all been for nothin'."

"So, you're going keep it."

"Right."

Roxy looked at Jane.

"I told you," Jane said. "I'm going along with Johnny."

"All right," Roxy said.

"You'll still do it?" Jane asked.

"Yes," Roxy said, "but like I said, only because Johnny stuck his neck out for me."

"Yes," Jane said, "he did."

"You'll be stickin' your neck out for me, now," Johnny said, "if you ride into Flagstaff alone. Hitch ain't gonna be there alone, you know."

"Well," Roxy said, "I'm just going to talk. And somehow, I can always get a man to talk to me."

Jane smiled.

"I bet you can."

"When are you leavin'?" Johnny asked.

"I'll ride out tomorrow morning," Roxy said. "If I push, I can get to Flagstaff tomorrow night."

"It's gotta be seventy miles," Johnny said.

"I'll push hard."

"Then you better get some rest," Jane suggested.

"You're right about that," Roxy said. "I'm going to finish this beer and go to my room. But first, you two have to promise me that you'll stay out of trouble while I'm gone."

"Believe me," Johnny said, "We're not gonna do anythin' to make ourselves noticeable. The last thing we want is Hitch comin' here while you're in Flagstaff."

"Don't worry," Roxy said, "we're not going to cross."

"But there's always the chance Hitch won't be there," Johnny said. "I mean, if he goes out himself, lookin' for me."

"I guess," Roxy said, "I'll find that out when I get there."

***

Roxy spent a quiet night in her room, and assumed that Johnny and Jane had done the same. In the morning she had an early breakfast alone, having already instructed the others to come down later, after she'd already left.

"When do you think you'll get back?" Jane had asked.

"Hopefully, I won't be gone more than a couple of days."

"And what if you don't come back?"

"If anything happens," Roxy said, "you'll probably hear about it."

"And what do we do?" Johnny asked.

"If you hear I've been killed," Roxy said, "then you'll probably have to start running again. If you hear Hitch was killed, then just stay here and wait. I'll be back."

"And if you're arrested?" Jane asked.

"If that happens, it should also make the news," Roxy reasoned. "You'll have to make up your own minds then."

They agreed.

During breakfast she thought it over again, in case she had something else to tell them before she left, but there was nothing.

Once she finished eating she went to the livery, collected her horse and left town, heading south to Flagstaff.

***

Jane woke the next morning lying in the crook of Johnny's arm, their naked bodies pressed together. The sex the night before had been energetic and had worn them both out. They went to sleep making a point of not talking about Roxy Doyle going to Flagstaff in the morning.

Jane rolled over and stared at the ceiling.

"What is it?" Johnny asked.

"I was just wondering if she left yet."

"I'm sure she did," Johnny said.

"Maybe we should've warned her."

"Maybe," Johnny said, also rolling onto his back, "we shouldn't have lied to her from the beginning."

"It's too late to worry about that now," Jane observed.

"Exactly," Johnny said, "just like it's too late to warn her before she rides out."

"So all we do now is . . . wait?" Jane asked.

"Wait," Johnny said, "and hope."

"If she gets herself killed—"

"—it's somethin' that's gonna happen to her sooner or later," Johnny said. "That's the kind of life she lives, isn't it?"

"I suppose so."

"This is our chance, Jane," he said. "Maybe our only chance."

"You're right," Jane said, "but I like her."

Johnny reached out and gathered her close, and soon she stopped talking about Roxy.

Chapter Thirty-Six

It was dusk when Roxy rode into Flagstaff, Arizona. The strain of piano music came down the street at her. Presumably from a saloon. She decided to follow the sound. It led her to a saloon with a big sign above the door: The Dutchman Saloon.

She tied her horse outside and went in. The piano was loud, as were the conversations going on. There was no stage, so she assumed there would be no dancing to go with the music. Two or three saloon girls were working the floor, wearing bright dresses. They were the only other women in the place, so when she entered she attracted attention.

She walked to the bar, where several men moved to make room for her.

"Thank you," she said.

"Buy you a drink?" one asked.

"I can buy my own," she replied, "but thanks for the offer."

"Just tryin' to be friendly," the man said.

"I appreciate that."

"Whataya have?" the barkeep asked.

"Beer."

He studied her for a moment, took in her gun and where it sat on her hip, then went for the beer. When he brought the glass, she picked it up and turned to the man who had offered to buy the drink. He was in his 30s, average height, dark-haired, nothing special, really.

"You always offer to buy strangers a drink?" she asked.

"Only pretty ones," he said, "but usually I do talk to strangers."

"Why is that?"

He moved his vest aside, showing her the star on his chest with SHERIFF written across it.

"Ah, I see."

"Sheriff Jeff Black."

"Roxy Doyle." Since she happened to walk right into the town lawman, she decided not to lie.

He smiled.

"I thought so, when you walked in. There aren't many women—red-haired women—who look like you and wear a gun the way you do."

"I suppose not."

"And you're obviously not tryin' to hide who you are," he commented.

"What would be the point?" she asked.

"Are you here lookin' for someone?" he asked.

"I am."

"Who?"

"A man named Hitch Moran."

Black frowned.

"That's not a good idea," he said.

"Why not?"

"He's not a pleasant man."

"I heard he was a bank robber," she said.

"Among other things," Black said, "although he hasn't robbed any banks around here."

"Is he wanted for anything else?" she asked. "Any of the 'other things' you referred to?"

"Not by me," he said. "Why do you want him?"

"Just to talk."

"Is that the truth?"

"Yes."

"You have a reputation, you know, of wantin' to do more than just talk."

"Reputations are exaggerated."

"Some are," he said, "some aren't. You sure you're not lookin' to plant him in the ground?"

"Now why would I want to do that?" she asked.

"Maybe you're lookin' for a bounty."

"I'm no bounty hunter," she said.

"What then? Revenge?"

"I just want to talk to him," she said, "that's all. Is he here?"

"In the saloon? No," the sheriff said. "But if you're askin' me if he's in town, the answer's yes. I don't think you'll have any trouble findin' him."

"Well," she said, putting her empty mug down, "there's no rush. I can find him tomorrow. Right now I've got to get myself and my horse some place to stay."

"There's a good livery stable at the end of Main Street," he told her. "And you'll pass a couple of decent hotels along the way."

"Thanks, Sheriff."

"You'll also pass my office," he added, "so you'll know where to find me, if you need me."

"I'll remember that. Thanks for the friendly greeting."

He shrugged.

"Just doin' my job," he said, "talkin' to strangers who come into town." He leaned closer. "Lettin' them know to keep out of trouble."

"Oh, I'll do that," she said. "I ain't here looking for trouble, you can depend on that."

"That's good to hear," Sheriff Black said. "Hard to believe, but good to hear."

Chapter Thirty-Seven

Roxy took her horse to the livery the sheriff told her about, then took her saddlebags and rifle to one of the hotels she had passed along the way. She got a room away from the main street.

In the room she saw and thought about the coincidence of running into the sheriff just moments after riding into town. And, of course, it was a coincidence, since there was no way he could have known she was coming. She had seen no telegraph wires on her way into town, so unless some sort of pony express brought the news . . .

At least she had found out from the sheriff that Hitch Moran was pretty well known in Flagstaff. What she didn't know was whether he was well-liked, or perhaps feared. If he was well-liked, he would have backing. If he was feared, he might even have more.

She would find out all her answers the next day.

***

Sheriff Jeff Black gave Roxy Doyle time to get herself situated before he left the Dutchman Saloon and walked to the other end of town. There he found Hitch Moran and some of his men seated at a table in the Royal Flush Saloon.

"What is she like?" Moran asked, when the sheriff told him that Roxy Doyle was in town looking for him.

"Beautiful," Jeff Black said, "confident, wears her gun like she knows how to use it."

"And what does she want with me?"

"She says she just wants to talk."

"About what?" Moran asked,

"We didn't get that far."

"So she's really the Lady Gunsmith?" Moran asked. "She really exists?"

"The only thing I didn't see was how she handles a gun," Sheriff Black said, "but yeah, it seems to be her."

"Well," Moran said, "Lady Gunsmith sure as hell doesn't have a reputation for talkin'."

"No, that's true," Black said.

"But?"

Sheriff Black shrugged.

"I think she's really here because she wants to talk to you," the lawman said.

"Okay, then," Hitch Moran said, "I'll talk to her."

"When?" Black asked.

"Whenever she finds me," Moran said. "And don't give 'er any help, Black. Let 'er find me herself. Got it?"

"I got it, Hitch."

"Now get out of here," Moran said. "Go make your rounds, or somethin'."

Sheriff Black got up and left. Moran had not even bought him a drink.

***

After the lawman left, Hitch Moran signaled to one of his men to come over to his table. Andy Davis left the bar and walked over, carrying two beers.

"Thanks," Moran said. "Siddown."

"What's going on?" Davis asked. "What'd the sheriff want?"

"Somebody rode into town today, says she's lookin' for me," Moran said.

"A girl?"

Moran nodded.

"What's she want?"

"He doesn't know," Moran said. "I'll have to talk to her to find out."

"Who is she?"

"Says her name is Roxy Doyle."

Davis, a plain looking man in his 30s, frowned.

"I know that—wait a minute. Ain't that the Lady Gunsmith?"

"Right."

Now Davis' eyebrows went up.

"If Lady Gunsmith is lookin' for you, how many reasons could there be?"

"You tell me."

"Well, one," Davis said. "She wants ta kill you."

"Why?"

"Why? Because you're Hitch Moran."

Moran grinned.

"You think that matters to her?" Moran asked. "You think she's gonna get a bigger reputation for killin' me?"

"Around here, yeah."

"Come on, Andy," Moran said. "I'm nobody. She's Lady Gunsmith."

Davis sniffed.

"That don't mean nothin' ta me."

"Get a look at her tomorrow," Moran said.

"Just a look?"

"Yeah," Moran said. "Don't approach her. I just want your opinion."

"On whether she's for real?"

"Yeah."

"Okay."

He started to get up.

"Wait."

Davis sat back down.

"What do we have on Johnny?"

"Not much," Davis said. "Still plenty of men out there lookin' for him."

"What about Bullhead City?"

"Why would he go back there?"

"Don't know," Moran said, "but that's where it all started, right?"

"Well, yeah."

"Send somebody over there," Moran said, "just for a check. Send two."

Davis looked over at the men at the bar.

"I'll send Henry and Karnes."

"Fine." Ian Henry and Benny Karnes had been with Moran for a few years. They knew Johnny Billings on sight. "If he's there just tell one of them to come back and tell me."

"Right."

"Be a damn sight easier if they'd finally get those telegraph lines in here."

"Yeah, it would."

"Okay," Moran said. "That's all."

Davis stood up.

"You gonna talk to 'er. Boss?"

"Why not?" Moran asked. "Seems to be the best way to find out what she wants, don't you think?"

"I dunno," Davis said. "I think I'd just kill 'er and be done with it."

"Andy," Moran said, "just be sure you do exactly as I tell you, and nothin' more. Got it?"

"I got it, boss."

Andy went back to the bar to talk to Henry and Karnes.

Chapter Thirty-Eight

Roxy came out of her hotel the next morning and immediately felt eyes on her. Not just the normal stares she attracted, but somebody watching her.

She made a show of looking both ways on the street, hoping it would appear she was looking for a store. She spotted the man across the street, lounging in a doorway, watching her. It was then she realized she needn't have bothered with any pretense. He wasn't hiding his interest. She assumed, then, that he had been sent by Hitch Moran.

That was fine with her. Let Moran take a look at her through the eyes of one of his men. She walked down the street until she came to a small restaurant, then went inside.

The few diners there gave Roxy and her gun a few looks, and then went back to their meals. She chose her own table which was, as usual, in the back. A middle-aged waitress took her order, brought her bacon-and-eggs and biscuits, with coffee.

"Can I get you anything else?" she asked.

"Can you sit for a minute?"

"Sure." The woman took the chair across from her. "What can I do for you?"

Roxy knew if bartenders heard most of what went on in a town, the next in line were probably waitresses.

"What can you tell me about Hitch Moran?"

The woman looked surprised, and suddenly wary.

"Why would you be interested in Hitch Moran?" she asked. "You ain't a bounty hunter, are you?"

"No, nothing like that," Roxy said, while she ate. "I just came here to talk to him, but I'd like to find out some things about him before that."

"What makes you think I'd know anythin'?" the woman asked.

"You're a waitress," Roxy said. "You hear things."

"Not about Hitch Moran." The woman stood up. "And if I do hear anythin' about him, I try to forget it right away. Listen Lady, if you want my advice, you'll forget about tryin' to talk to him."

She turned and went back to the kitchen. Her reaction had been intense, but while she did seem to know him, Roxy did not get the impression she was afraid of Moran.

She finished her breakfast, and when the waitress came to give her the check and collect the money, she acted as if they had never spoken about Moran.

Roxy left the small restaurant and saw the man across the street, still watching her. She decided to cross over and have a word with him. Unfortunately, he had other plans.

He ran.

***

Andy Davis picked Lady Gunsmith up outside her hotel, followed her to the café. He thought she had seen him watching, but she hadn't made a move against him. However, when she came out after having breakfast, she suddenly started crossing the street to him. His instructions were not to have any contact with her, so he did the only thing he could think of—he ran.

He looked behind him as he ran off, didn't see her following him. He knew where Hitch Moran had his breakfast every day, a small café a block away from the Dutchman Saloon. Since he wasn't being followed, he headed directly there.

***

Moran looked up over his ham steak-and-eggs, saw Andy Davis come into the café, breathing heavily.

"What went wrong?" he asked, as Andy sat.

"What makes ya think somethin' went wrong?"

"You ran here, Andy," Horan said. "Here, relax, have a cup of coffee, and tell me what happened."

"Nothin' happened," Davis said picking up the coffee. "I watched her, like you said, and didn't talk to her. It was only when she came toward me that I ran."

"Straight here," Moran said.

"Yeah, that's right," Davis said. "She wasn't followin' me."

"You better be right about that."

"I am." He drank his coffee as his breathing slowed down.

"So, what do you think?" Moran asked.

"She's beautiful, all right," Davis said, "and she don't seem clumsy with that gun on her hip."

"Did she talk to anybody this mornin'?"

"Not that I saw," Davis said. "Maybe the desk clerk at the hotel, or the waitress at the café."

"Which café?"

"Just down the street from her hotel."

"And which hotel is she in?"

"The Sundown."

"So the waitress would be . . ."

". . . Marjorie, yeah," Davis said.

"Marjorie wouldn't have told her anythin'," Moran said.

"That's what I thought."

"And the hotel clerk doesn't know nothin'," Moran said. "Okay, Andy. You can go."

"And what should I do?"

"Get some sleep, or some breakfast, whatever," Moran said. "Just stay away from that woman."

"And you?"

"I'll talk to her," Moran said, "as soon as she finds me."

Chapter Thirty-Nine

Roxy entered the sheriff's office, found the man sitting behind the desk with his feet up. He dropped them to the floor when he saw her.

"Miss Doyle," he said. "What can I do for you this mornin'?"

"You can tell me where to find Hitch Moran."

"What makes you think I'd know that?"

"There was a man following me this morning," she said. "I'm assuming he works for Moran. And for Moran to have sent a man to keep an eye on me, somebody had to tell him I was looking for him. And since you're the only one I talked to about him, that would be you."

Sheriff Black stared at Roxy, looking as if he had been caught with his hand in the cookie jar.

"Oops," he said. smiling.

"I'm not mad," she said. "I just need to find him, and you can make things easier on me."

"Well," the lawman said, "I can probably tell you a few places he might be—"

"No, what I'd like you to do is introduce us."

"What? Why?"

"Because with you there, that should make sure there's no gun play."

Black thought about it, then said, “Huh, you might be right about that.”

“So? Where is he?”

“There are a few places he might be,” the lawman said, “but let’s try the Flush.”

“The what?”

“The Royal Flush Saloon,” Black said, standing up. “That’s where he usually is. Come on, I’ll take you over.”

They left the office, with him taking the lead.

***

“This is a rundown part of town,” Sheriff Black told her, as they walked down the street towards the saloon. “The town council’s talkin’ about maybe doin’ somethin’ to clean it up.”

“Pretty fancy name for a saloon on this street,” Roxy observed.

“Like I said,” Black answered, “it’s rundown now, but it wasn’t always.”

When they reached the saloon, Black stopped and turned to her.

“Before we go in I gotta tell you, the customers here ain’t the nicest you’ll ever find. There may be some . . . remarks made.”

“I can handle that,” Roxy told him.

"Yeah, I guess you can," Black said. "Okay, let's go in."

"It's a little early, isn't it?" she asked.

"With this place, it don't matter."

They went through the batwing doors, one of which squeaked as it swung back and forth. The inside seemed as dirty to Roxy as the outside, and the men who were at the bar, or at some of the tables, fit right in.

There were 3 men at the bar, though, who were a bit cleaner, and Black approached them.

"Hey boys," he said, "any of you seen Hitch this mornin'?"

"Hey sweetheart," one of the men at a table called, "what're ya doin' with the law? Come on over here and we'll show you a good time."

Roxy ignored him.

"Who's askin', Sheriff?" one of the 3 asked. "You or her?"

"Let's say I'm askin' for her, Rafe."

"This that gal wants to talk to him?" one of the other asked. "Claims she's Lady Gunsmith?"

"My name's Roxy Doyle," she said. "That's all I'm laying claim to."

"That ain't what we heard," Rafe said. "Seems like you might be aimin' to shoot Hitch."

"That's not my intention," she said. "I just want to talk to him."

"About what?" Rafe asked.

"That's between me and him," she said.

"Well," Rafe said, "he ain't here, and we don't know when he will be."

The sheriff looked at Roxy.

"Whataya wanna do, wait?" he asked.

She thought it over, while the men in the place kept staring at her, and the one in the back kept making remarks and kissing noises.

"No," she said. "Let's move on." She looked at Rafe. "If he comes in, tell him I was here looking for him."

"It would help if you was to tell us why you're lookin' for him," Rafe said. "Then we could tell him and he could decide if he wantsta see you."

She thought it over again, then decided the truth wouldn't hurt, since they didn't know where Johnny was.

"Tell him it's about Johnny Billings," she said, "and Bullhead City."

She turned and walked out, the sheriff hurrying to catch up.

Chapter Forty

"Why didn't you tell me?" the sheriff demanded, when he caught up.

"Tell you what?"

"That you were here representing John Billings," Black said.

"Why? Is that a problem?"

"If you want there to be no gun play with Hitch Moran, it is," the sheriff explained.

"Is that so?"

"This changes everything!" Sheriff Black said, as they walked back toward the better part of town.

"Why?"

"Because Hitch Moran wants Johnny Billings dead," the lawman said. "After . . ."

"After?"

". . . after he gets what's owed him."

"The money from the Bullhead City bank robbery?" she asked.

"You know about that?"

"I know Moran robbed the bank, and Billings stole the money from him."

"And that's all you know?"

She stopped walking.

"Is there more?"

"Well . . . no," he said, "not that I'd tell you, anyway. I'll leave that to Hitch—if he doesn't kill you, first. Or you kill him."

"That's why you're going to be there, to keep the peace," she reminded him. "You said there were other places he might be?"

"The Flush was the most likely," Black said, "but we could check a few others. But when we find him I'd be very careful how I told him that you were here on John Billings' behalf."

"Were they . . . friends?" Roxy asked, wondering just how much there was that she didn't know.

"I'll leave that to him," he said. "This way."

***

After 3 other places—2 saloons and a restaurant—Roxy got the feeling Sheriff Black was giving her the runaround.

"Sheriff," she said, as they left the 4th saloon of the day, "while I appreciate your help, I think I'll take it from here, myself."

"But . . . there are a few other places."

"I know, you've said," she commented, "but I think I'm going to stick with the Royal Flush Saloon. Eventually, he'll show up there."

"But . . . you're goin' back there alone?"

"Yes, I am."

"But . . . it ain't safe."

"You're right," she said. "It's not safe, for anybody who wants to get in my way."

"Now wait—"

"You've been running me around town all morning, Sheriff," she said. "It's time for you to go back to your job, and let me go back to what I came here to do."

"Kill Moran?"

"I told you," she said, "I'm here to talk to him."

Black made a face.

"I'm findin' that just a little hard to believe."

"Well then," she said, "I guess you'll have to wait and see."

"Miss Doyle—"

"If you hear any shooting from that part of town," she said. "just know that I didn't start it—"

"Miss—"

"—but if anyone does," she went on, "I'll be the one to finish it." She started to walk away, then turned and added, "And that you can believe."

Chapter Forty-One

Roxy was no longer being watched, so she decided to do the watching. She positioned herself across the street from the Royal Flush.

***

While Roxy was standing across the street from the Royal Flush Saloon, Hitch Moran was having breakfast in the café where Marjorie worked.

"I didn't tell her anything," the waitress told Hitch. "I didn't know who she was."

"And she didn't say?"

"No."

"And?"

"And nothing," Marjorie said. "She asked me to sit for a minute, but when she mentioned your name, I got up and left. We didn't talk again."

"Not even when she paid her bill?"

"No."

Hitch stared at her. Once she was in love with him, but now she just feared him.

"Okay, Marjorie." He stood up and dropped some money on the table. "Thanks."

He left and headed back to the Flush.

***

It was difficult for Roxy Doyle to go unnoticed, so she had to find a very good hiding place. Luckily, there was a hardware store with plenty of crates and barrels out front. She hid behind them and watched as several men entered and left the Royal Flush. The problem was, she didn't know what Hitch looked like. She should have asked the sheriff, but truth was she got tired of talking to the man.

"Can I help you?" a male voice asked.

She turned and saw a young man wearing a long white, but smudged apron, looking at her from the doorway of the hardware store.

"Do you work here?"

He was young, and his eyes were wide as he stared at the beautiful redhead.

"Uh, yeah."

"What's your name?"

"Danny."

"Well, Danny, maybe you can help me," she said. "Do you know what a man named Hitch Moran looks like?"

"Uh, yeah, I do."

"Well, I don't," she said, "and I'm looking for him. So you could do me a favor and go across the street to see if he's in that saloon. And then come back here and tell me what he looks like. Can you do that?"

"Sure. I can do that."

"I don't have much money, but I can give you—"

"You don't need to give me nothin', Miss," he said. "Just wait here."

The boy, who couldn't have been more than 18, ran across the street, still wearing his apron, and peered over the batwing doors of the Royal Flush. He was there briefly, and then ran back.

"He's in there," he said. "He's wearing a blue shirt, and sittin' with two of his friends."

"Thanks, Danny."

"Are you goin' in there?" Danny asked.

"I am."

"That ain't a place for a lady, Miss."

"Do I look like a lady?" she asked.

Danny looked her up and down, gun and all, and said, "You sure do!"

"You're cute," she said to him, stroking his cheek. He hadn't even started to shave, yet. "Maybe when I'm done across the street you and me will get better acquainted.

She left him standing there with his mouth open and started across.

***

"What did Marjorie say to her?" Andy Davis asked Hitch.

"Not much," Hitch said. "She says she didn't tell Doyle anythin'. What about Henry and Karnes?"

"They're on their way to Bullhead City right now," Davis assured him.

Hitch looked at the other man, Evans, who was just sitting there drinking.

"What've you got to say?"

"Huh? Wha—"

It took Larry Evans a moment to realize he was being spoken to.

"Never mind," Hitch said. "Just shut up."

"Boss," Davis said.

"What?"

Davis indicated the front doors. Hitch looked that way and saw a redhaired woman wearing a gun enter the Royal Flush. She looked around, spotted him, and started over.

"Looks like she found ya," Davis said.

Chapter Forty-Two

Roxy saw the only man in the place wearing a blue shirt and walked over to his table. He was handsome, in his 30s, and appeared very relaxed while watching her approach.

"Are you Hitch Moran?"

"That's right. And you're Roxy Doyle?"

"That's right."

"I heard you were lookin' for me," Hitch said. "I wondered when you'd find me. Boys, give us some room."

"Uh, boss, don't you think—"

"Give the lady some room, Andy," Hitch said, cutting him off. "Let her sit. And take this idiot with you."

"Huh? Wha—" Evans started.

"Go!" Hitch snapped.

The two men stood up and went to the bar.

"And bring two beers over here!" he called.

"Have a seat, Miss Doyle," Hitch said. "You can tell me what's on your mind."

"Thanks," Roxy said, and sat down.

Davis returned with two beers, set them down and went back to the bar.

"On me," Hitch said, picking his up.

Roxy nodded, picked hers up left handed—as she noticed he had—and took a sip.

"So," Hitch said, "what's Lady Gunsmith got against me?"

"Nothing, personally," she said. "I'm here on behalf of someone else—someone you're looking for."

"And who would that be?"

"Johnny Billings."

Hitch stared at her for a few moments, then started laughing loudly.

"And I suppose Jane is with him?" he asked.

"That's right," she said. "They're afraid you're looking for him to kill him."

"They're right," Hitch said. "So they sent you to kill me first?"

"I told them my gun's not for hire," she said. "I said I'd come and talk to you."

"Well, that's real odd."

"Why?"

"They must've known I'd tell you the truth." He frowned. "Or maybe they thought you'd kill me first." He pointed his finger at her and raised his eyebrows. "I know. They thought we'd try to kill each other on sight, and you'd never find out the truth."

"And what truth is that, Hitch?" she asked.

"Did they tell you about the bank robbery?"

She nodded.

"In Bullhead City, right?"

"What did they tell you about it?"

"That you and your men robbed the bank there, and that Johnny stole the money from you."

Hitch sipped his beer again and set it down.

"They almost told you the truth," he observed.

"Almost?"

Hitch sat back, looked over at the bar.

"Andy!"

Davis came over.

"This is Roxy Doyle," he said. "This is my man, Andy Davis."

Davis nodded at her, and she returned it.

"Tell Miss Doyle about Bullhead City," Hitch said.

"Well," he said, "it's a growin' town—"

"The bank," Hitch said, "tell her about the bank."

"The bank job?"

"Andy," Hitch said, "just tell her what happened."

"We robbed the bank," Andy said. "Cleaned it out good. Didn't even have to deal with a law, because we knew the sheriff and his deputies were out of town."

"How did you know that?"

"We sent somebody into town to look everythin' over," Davis said. "The town, the bank, the law."

"So somebody knew what they were doing," she said.

"Oh yeah," Davis said, "it was planned perfect."

She looked at Hitch.

"So now I know how smart you are," she said. "Is that it?"

"Oh, it wasn't me who planned the job," Hitch said.

"Who, then?"

"Tell 'er, Andy."

"It was Johnny," Davis said. "Johnny Billings. He was the brains."

Roxy felt the sting of those word and looked at Hitch.

"Is that true?"

"It is," he said, "and that's not all. Andy?"

"After the job," Davis said. "Johnny and his woman stole the money. All of it. And they let it be known that the Hitch Moran gang robbed the bank."

"So if you're wanted in Arizona, how can you sit here?"

"Sheriff Black?" Hitch asked, laughing. "We don't have to worry about him. Besides, it's just a rumor Johnny spread. There's no proof."

"So you're telling me that Johnny Billings planned the job, you and your men pulled it off, and then he stole all the money?"

"Exactly." He looked at Davis. "That's all, Andy."

"Why should I believe you?"

"Do you believe everythin' Johnny told you?" he asked. "And Jane?"

"No," Roxy said. "Jane lied to me from the beginning."

"Ah! See? That's what they do. They lied to all of us, and I aim to find them and make them pay."

"By killing them?"

"I've robbed banks," he said, "and stagecoaches, a train or two. But I ain't never killed anybody."

She took a moment to absorb that. She had the feeling Hitch was telling the truth, and she already had proof that Jane and Johnny would lie to get what they want.

"Tell me something," she said. "Can Johnny handle a gun?"

"Oh," Hitch said, "that's something he can't do. He's terrible with a gun. Why, did he tell you different?"

"No," she said, "when it came to that he told me the truth."

"And," Hitch said, "probably only that."

Chapter Forty-Three

Roxy's head was spinning as she tried to put it all into prospective. Johnny and Jane were proven liars. She knew nothing about Hitch Moran except that he admitted to being a bandit. But not a killer.

"I'll make a deal with you," Hitch said. "Take me to Johnny. I'll get the money back and give you an even share."

"I don't want a share," she said. "That's not why I'm here."

"No," he said, "you're here because Johnny and Jane lied to you. Because they figured you'd kill me for them. Or maybe that we'd kill each other."

"If they have the money, and sent me here to kill you, what makes you think they'll still be where I left them?"

"Because they're gonna want to hear from you if you managed to kill me," he said. "They'll want to know they don't need to run anymore."

"They're running because they think you'll kill them," Roxy said. "Why would they think that if you're not a killer?"

"I never said I wasn't a killer," Hitch replied. "I said that during my robberies, I've never killed anyone. There's a difference."

"Tell me what the difference is," Roxy said.

"There's no point in killing someone during a robbery," Hitch said. "It's only money—until you kill somebody. But when somebody crosses me, or threatens me, that's different. Don't you see that? Come on, you see that. You've done it."

"I kill people who are trying to kill me."

"And so do I."

They sat and stared at each other.

"So where does that leave us?" Hitch asked.

"I don't know."

"In the street, facing each other?" Hitch asked. "Then, if you kill me, you can tell Johnny he's free."

"If you're telling me the truth," Roxy said, "I won't allow them to keep that money."

"So help me get it back."

"I intend to take it back where it came from," she said, starting to rise. "The Bullhead City Bank."

"No problem," Hitch said, sitting. "I'll just take it again. And this time I won't have to deal with Johnny Billings."

She stood up.

"I'm not going to kill him," she said.

He spread his hands.

"Neither am I," Hitch said. "I might just be content with the idea that he'll always be running from me, looking over his shoulder. If you tell him anything, tell him I'll always be looking for him."

She nodded, even though she wasn't sure what she was going to tell Johnny and Jane Billings.

She figured Hitch was telling her the truth but, as with Johnny and Jane, it was only part of the truth.

Everyone was lying to her, one way or another, she thought, as she walked out of the Royal Flush. But nobody was going to keep that money. That was the way she figured she could punish all of them.

***

"Boss," Andy Davis said, after Roxy left. "She ain't the killer everybody says she is, huh?"

"I didn't wanna find out, Andy," Hitch said. "So I told her enough truth to confuse her."

"So what will she do now?"

"She'll go back to Johnny."

"And?"

Hitch looked up at him.

"Get me Mohave Sam."

"That redskin? For what?"

"He can track a snake," Hitch said. "I want him to track a Lady Gunsmith."

Chapter Forty-Four

Roxy wasn't sure what to do next.

Did she believe enough of what Hitch Moran had told her to ride back to Tuba City and confront Johnny and Jane with it? Or did she need more information? And if she did, where was she going to get it?

She could leave town, ride to Tuba City and have it out with them.

Or she could ride to Bullhead City and see if she could find out the truth there.

She knew what Clint Adams would do. He had contacts all over the West. He would send out telegrams and get the answers. She didn't have those contacts. She had him, but by the time she found him it might be too late. Johnny and Jane might be gone, even if they were waiting for her to come back, they might decide to leave, taking the money with them.

The money.

That was what made the decision for her.

She couldn't allow Johnny and Jane to ride off with that money. Not until she knew the truth.

She decided not to even wait until morning. She headed for the hotel to check out, and then she'd get her horse from the livery and ride.

***

"Boss."

Hitch looked up at Andy.

"What now?"

"I just got word Doyle checked out of her hotel."

"Where'd she go?"

"I don't kn—"

"Check the livery stables," Hitch said. "I want to know if she left town, and if she did, which way she went."

"Right."

"And where's Sam?"

"He's on his way."

"He better be!"

***

Roxy rode out of Flagstaff and headed north. It was less than 80 miles to Tuba City. She only hoped that when she got there, Johnny and Jane were still there. She was going to take the money from them and make them tell her the truth.

***

When Andy Davis walked back into the Royal Flush, Mohave Sam was sitting with Hitch. The Indian was not only an expert tracker, but a killer, as well.

"So?"

"She took her horse out of the livery and rode out."

"Which way did she go?"

"That I can't find out," Davis said.

"What?"

"The guy at the livery didn't watch her ride out."

"A woman who looks like her and he didn't watch her ride out?" Hitch asked.

"Boss," Davis said, "he's like a hundred years old."

Hitch looked at Mohave Sam,

"She's either going to Bullhead City, or someplace else. I need to know."

Sam nodded, stood up and left the saloon.

"How's he gonna find out?" Davis asked.

"Don't worry, he will," Hitch said. "Who do we have in town?"

"You, me, Evans, Sam, a few other guys—"

"Get 'em all here," Hitch said. "Now!"

"Right."

***

By the time Mohave Sam got back to the Royal Flush, all of Hitch's men were there.

"Well?" Hitch asked.

Sam pointed.

"North?"

The Indian nodded.

"Tuba City?" Hitch asked.

The Indian shrugged.

"Okay," Hitch said, standing up, "let's go. Sam, you take the lead."

The Indian nodded, and they filed out into the street and onto their horses.

***

It occurred to Johnny Billings only that morning that maybe he and Jane ought to leave Tuba City.

"And go where?" Jane asked, as he broached the subject at breakfast.

"Someplace safe."

"And where would that be?" she asked. "We're not gonna be safe until Hitch is dead."

"So you wanna wait for Roxy?" he asked.

"Maybe she'll be back today or tomorrow."

"Maybe," Johnny said. "If she did her goddamned job."

Chapter Forty-Five

Roxy road hard and made Tuba City by dusk. But her horse paid the price.

"This animal is done in," the man said at the livery.

"I'll get a new one before I leave town."

"I ain't got any to sell," he said. "I don't know where ya gonna get one."

"I'll take that one," she said, pointing to the horse Johnny Billings had been riding.

"That belongs to somebody else," the man complained.

"Not anymore," Roxy said. "Put my saddle on it."

"You ridin' out in the dark?"

"Just as soon as I can."

She left the livery and headed for the hotel, where she'd left Johnny and Jane.

***

"Mohave Sam says she's definitely going to Tuba City, and her horse is about done," Hitch said to his men. "So we're gonna pick up the pace."

"Where is Sam?" Davis asked.

"He's gone up ahead," Hitch said, "to make sure she don't change direction on us."

"You think she knows we're followin' her?" Davis asked.

"If it hasn't occurred to her," Hitch said, "then she ain't as smart as I thought she was."

***

Roxy figured if Hitch wasn't tracking her himself, he probably sent somebody else. But the part of his story she believed was about Johnny planning the job and stealing the money. After all, Johnny had already admitted to stealing the money. So she figured she had at least an hour to get the money away from Johnny and Jane, after which she could leave them to their business with Hitch. If they wanted each other dead, that was fine, but she wasn't planning on getting in the middle.

When she knocked on their room door there was no answer. That suited her. She got the door open, went inside, and took care of her business. Then she left the hotel and started walking around Tuba City, looking for a likely place for them to eat.

***

When Mohave Sam arrived in Tuba City, he immediately noticed Roxy Doyle walking the street. There was no mistaking her, not with her red hair, the way she wore her gun, and how beautiful she was.

Although Sam was an Indian, he was an expert at blending into the background. He watched her.

***

She found them in a small restaurant, foolishly sitting at a table by the front window.

"This is not a good place to sit," she told them, as soon as she entered.

"Roxy!" Jane said. "I'm so glad to see you."

"Why are you sitting at the window?"

"We wanted to keep an eye out for you," Johnny said.

"And get yourselves shot."

"Is he dead?" Jane asked. "Did you kill Hitch?"

"No," Roxy said, looking at her, "I didn't."

Jane's face fell.

"Why not?"

"Because that's what you both wanted me to do," Roxy said, "kill him. Not talk to him."

"What did he tell you?" Johnny asked. "You can't listen to him, he's a liar—"

"So are the two of you," Roxy said. "Liars. We've established that."

"Well, sit down," Johnny said. "You must be tired. Let's talk."

"You planned the job, didn't you, Johnny?" she asked. "And all along you planned to steal the money from Hitch."

"Look," Johnny said, "if that's what he told you—"

"He told me a few things," Roxy said, "but I think that's the only part I believe."

"Why would you believe anything he says?" Jane asked.

"Because," Roxy said, "everybody lies."

"I told you why I did that," Jane complained.

"Yes, because you were a desperate wife," Roxy said. The other diners in the restaurant started to watch. "So now I'll give you something to really be desperate about."

"What are you talking about?" Johnny asked.

"I'm taking that money back to the Bullhead City Bank," Roxy told them.

They both froze, and then Johnny said, "What?"

Roxy didn't answer. She walked out the front door. Johnny and Jane got up quickly and followed her, causing a waiter to run out, grab Johnny and insist that he pay for the meal.

Jane followed Roxy down the darkening street while Johnny shoved money at the man.

"You can't do that," Jane said. "You couldn't."

"Watch me."

"The money is in our room," Jane said.

"It *was* in your room," Roxy said. "It's not, anymore."

Johnny heard that as he caught up and he said, "I don't believe you."

"I know," Roxy said, "that's because everybody lies, but I'm not lying now. And I'll tell you another thing. I'm sure Hitch Moran is either right behind me, or he sent somebody."

"No!" Jane cried.

"I knew we shoulda left town!" Johnny said.

"Are you sure?" Jane asked.

"I am," Roxy said, "because there's been a man watching me. He's an Indian. That mean anything to you?"

"Mohave Sam," Johnny said, crestfallen. "Hitch won't be far behind." He grabbed Jane. "We gotta get outta town!"

"But Roxy has the money," Jane cried.

"We'll see."

Johnny ran for his hotel.

Chapter Forty-Six

Roxy walked to the livery with Jane on her heels.

"No, no, you can't leave yet!"

"I've got to," Roxy said. "I don't want to be here when Hitch arrives."

"Then we have to leave with you."

"You're not riding with me anymore," Roxy said. "Besides, Johnny doesn't have a horse. I took it."

"You're leavin' us to die?" Jane demanded.

"I'm leaving you to do what you should've done a long time ago," Roxy said. "Face Hitch."

"He'll kill Johnny!"

Roxy led the horse outside. Her saddlebags were much thicker than they had been when she arrived.

"Look on the bright side," Roxy said. "He might not kill you."

She started her horse up the street with Jane running behind her. Then, ahead of her, she saw Johnny run into the street and wave his arms.

"You gotta stop!" he cried. "Jane, she's got our money."

Roxy wondered who the law was in Tuba City and when he would put in an appearance.

She also noticed Johnny was wearing his gun. According to Hitch, he couldn't use it, but that could have been another lie. Johnny could have been faking. She couldn't take a chance.

"I said stop!" Johnny cried, dropping his hand to his side.

There was very little light now, except what was coming from a couple of saloons, and a few street lamps in the middle of town.

"Don't do it, Johnny," she said.

"Johnny, don't!" Jane shouted.

"I gotta," Johnny said.

"You're not going to leave me a choice, Johnny," Roxy said.

"Roxy—" he said, but then he staggered as something struck him in the back. He fell to his knees, tried to reach behind him, then went to his hands and knees.

"Johnny!" Jane screamed.

There was a knife sticking out from his left shoulder.

Roxy watched the Indian she assumed was Mohave Sam walk out of the shadows and up to Johnny.

"He is not dead," he said. "I did not want you to kill him before Hitch got here."

"I've got no beef with you, Indian," she said. "Don't make me kill you."

"I know you have the money," Sam said, "but I cannot stop you. I have no gun. But Hitch—"

"When Hitch arrives, you tell him I'm on my way to Bullhead City to return the money."

Jane reached Johnny and knelt beside him.

"He will try to stop you," the Indian said.

"I know."

Jane looked up at Roxy.

"You can't leave us."

"Just watch me," Roxy said, and rode around the 3 of them.

***

She rode into Bullhead City five days later. Again, she had pushed the horse she was riding to the point where she would probably need a new one. But she couldn't take the chance that Hitch and his men would beat her there.

Riding out of Tuba City into the dark had been harrowing, since she didn't know the terrain that well. She took her time, hoping her new horse would not step in a chuckhole. When first light came she was dead tired, but continued to ride, pushing the horse harder.

She had to camp at night, and sleep lightly, in case they caught up to her, but she knew Hitch would take the time to deal with Johnny and Jane. She was fairly certain she would reach Bullhead City before they did.

***

Of course, what Roxy didn't know was that Hitch had already sent two men—Henry and Karnes—to Bullhead City, telling them to intercept her before she got to the bank.

As she rode up to the bank, two men rose from the chairs they had been sitting in and stood between her and the bank door.

"How'd you get here ahead of me?" she asked.

Karnes laughed.

"We was already here, looking for Johnny."

"And," Roxy said, "Hitch told you I'd be coming."

"That's right," Henry said. "Now, you better get down and hand over that money."

Roxy sat taller in her saddle.

"I don't think so."

"Don't make us take it," Karnes advised.

"You can't take it," Roxy said. "There are only two of you."

Henry laughed.

"You're a girl," he said. "We don't care what your reputation says. You're a girl."

"I've heard that from a lot of men," she said. "Now get out of the way."

"We can't do that," Henry said.

"If we let you by, Hitch will kill us," Karnes said.

"And if you try to stop me, I will," Roxy said. "It's your choice. At least if you let me by now and live, you can get away before Hitch gets here."

Both men wet their lips nervously. For all their talk about her being a girl, they were having second thoughts.

"Well?" she snapped.

One man jerked, startled, and then both men slowly started to walk away.

She dismounted, took down her saddlebags, and carried them into the bank.

***

Weeks later—while she was back on the trail of her father, Gavin Doyle—she saw a news story in a newspaper about the Hitch Moran gang being gunned down while trying to rob the Bullhead City Bank. Stopping in to warn the sheriff there had been a good move on her part. The law had been ready for Hitch Moran's second robbery.

She never did find out what happened to Johnny and Jane Billings. But she knew one thing. Never again would she be taken in by a desperate wife.

Coming Spring 2019

Lady Gunsmith 7
Roxy Doyle and the James Boys

Gavin Doyle has reportedly been seen around St. Joseph, Missouri. Once there, Roxy spots a man who someone tells her is "Thomas Howard." But she knows the man by his real name—Jesse James. She had been introduced to Jesse by Belle Starr some time ago, and had also had a tryst with his brother, Frank. Jesse's looking for reliable people to form a new gang…

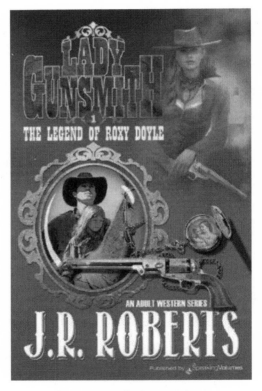

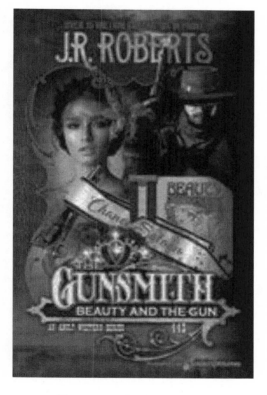

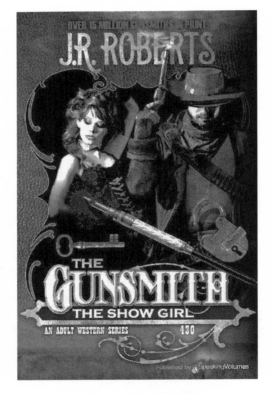

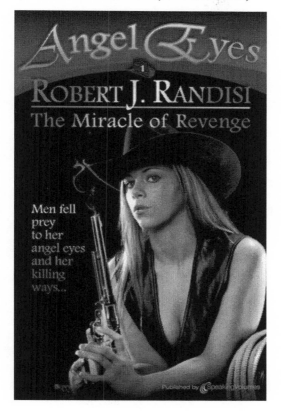

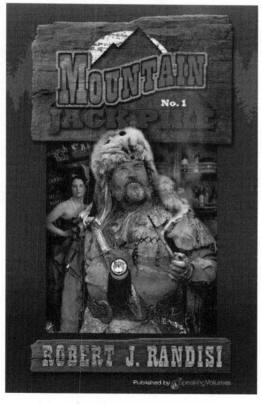

Made in the USA
Coppell, TX
26 November 2019